STO✓

FRIEN OF ACPL

W9-BBG-940

j
DeC
Monke

DO NOT REMOVE
CARDS FROM POCKET

ALLEN COUNTY PUBLIC LIBRARY

FORT WAYNE, INDIANA 46802

You may return this book to any agency, branch,
or bookmobile of the Allen County Public Library.

DEMCO

Monkey See.
Monkey Do.

Also by Barthe DeClements

Nothing's Fair in Fifth Grade

Sixth Grade Can Really Kill You

How Do You Lose Those Ninth Grade Blues?

Seventeen and In-Between

I Never Asked You to Understand Me

Double Trouble

No Place for Me

The Fourth Grade Wizards

Five-Finger Discount

Elkhart County Public Li
Elkhart, Indiana

Monkey See.
Monkey Do.

Barthe DeClements

**Delacorte
Press**

Allen County Public Library
Ft. Wayne, Indiana

Published by
Delacorte Press
Bantam Doubleday Dell Publishing Group, Inc.
666 Fifth Avenue
New York, New York 10103

Copyright © 1990 by Barthe DeClements

All rights reserved. No part of this book may be reproduced or
transmitted in any form or by any means, electronic or mechanical,
including photocopying, recording or by any information storage
and retrieval system, without the written permission of the Publisher,
except where permitted by law.

The trademark Delacorte Press® is registered in the U.S. Patent and
Trademark Office.

Library of Congress Cataloging in Publication Data

DeClements, Barthe.
    Monkey see. Monkey do. / by Barthe DeClements.
        p.   cm.
    Summary: Jerry's adored father seems unable to stay out of jail,
causing the sixth-grader anguish at home and in school.
    ISBN 0-385-30158-8
    [1. Fathers and sons—Fiction. 2. Prisoners' families—Fiction.]
    I. Title.
    PZ7.D3584Mo   1990
    [Fic]—dc20   89-71482
                                                            CIP
                                                            AC

Manufactured in the United States of America

October 1990

10 9 8 7 6 5 4 3 2 1

BVG

This book is dedicated to my brother, Roger,
and to my son, Roger, two shining knights in my life.

I wish to acknowledge the debt I owe to my daughter, Nicole Southard, for critiquing the manuscript, and to my son, Christopher Greimes, for editing it. I wish also to thank Nancy Wilson, who made me feel welcome in her school, and Kris Kellogg and her students, whose activities and suggestions are a part of this story.

Contents

1

Cops and Robbers

I stood by the front door listening. Nobody was supposed to be inside. My dad was supposed to be working at the tire store and my mom was supposed to be at Patrick's Grill. And there shouldn't be a strange car in front of our house either.

But there were sounds. I heard them. And laughter. Dad's laughter! And Rattler's growly voice.

My dad knew it was a parole violation to associate with anyone who'd been in prison. He could get sent back to the reformatory for seeing Rattler. How could he be so dumb? And what was he doing home in the afternoon?

I inched the door open. There was Dad with Rattler, slouching on the couch drinking beer and smoking cigarettes. When he saw me, he jumped to his feet and put his arm around my shoulders. "Ah, my boy! You're home from school. You remember Rattler, your old friend?"

I nodded. "Ya, hi."

Rattler put his beer down and stood up to shake my hand. "Still got your old man's brown eyes and gap-

1

toothed grin, I see. But you're getting to be a monster. How old are you now, Jerry? Twelve?"

"Not until next month," I told him.

He gave my back a slap. "You sure have grown."

He sure had shrunk. I remember my dad always referred to him as a runt, but I didn't remember his being this small.

"You're almost as tall as Rattler," Dad said.

"But not as strong." Rattler shoved up the sleeve of his sweater, crooked his arm, and made his biceps bounce up and down.

"Did they have a weight room in your joint?" Dad asked him.

"Naw. They didn't have nothin'. I did push-ups on the concrete floor and chin-ups on the bars." He gave me another slap. "You can always beat 'em, kid."

I smiled and nodded some more. "I guess I'll get something to eat."

Rattler sat back on the couch and picked up his beer. I headed toward the kitchen thinking that two and a half years in prison wasn't exactly beating them. There were chicken slices in a doggie bag in the fridge. I made myself a sandwich, grabbed a can of Pepsi, and went out the back door to my tree house.

I'd built the tree house a little over a year ago when Mom and I first came to Snohomish. We'd moved here so she could be near my dad, who was still in the Monroe reformatory. After Dad was released, he and I swore on the North Star that we would never steal again. He'd gotten all shook up when I told him I'd shoplifted sandals for Mom's Christmas present.

Mom has varicose veins bulging out of her legs.

2

She's a waitress and was teetering around on high heels from two o'clock in the afternoon to ten o'clock at night. I thought the sandals would make her legs feel better. All they did was make me feel guilty.

Having been around Dad, I guess my stealing was a case of monkey see monkey do. Only as soon as I stole the sandals I couldn't stand the thought of being a thief. I hadn't clipped a thing since Dad and I had made that pact on the North Star. I didn't think he had either, but I wasn't sure if he'd changed inside. I worried that if he got around his old buddies, he might drop into his old ways.

In fact, I was so busy worrying that Grace startled me when her head popped through the hole in the tree house floor. "What're you doing?" she asked.

"Just thinking," I said, wiping my hands on my pants. "Come on up. How come you weren't on the bus?"

"Mom had a PTA meeting. I rode home with her." Grace had a smile on her face as she settled cross-legged in front of me.

I poked the tab into my pop can. "So, your new teacher must be all right."

"All right!" She bugged her blue eyes at me. "Mr. Brewster humiliated me in front of the whole class."

"And you're smiling?"

"I'm smiling because my mom's going to school tomorrow to see about getting me out of his room."

"What exactly did you do, PK?" I call Grace "PK" sometimes, especially when she acts like the preacher's kid she is.

"I didn't do anything. Nothing! Nothing anyone

3

else wouldn't do when they meet their friends after a whole summer. What did *you* do when you saw Pete?"

"Oh, we slapped hands and stuff."

"Right! Only I didn't get to do 'stuff.' Mari and I were hugging each other when Mr. Brewster started yelling at us. The bell hadn't even rung. We sat down for him anyway.

"Then the idiot put us in alphabetical order. Who sits in alphabetical order in the sixth grade? I bet your class doesn't."

"No," I said automatically. It was hard for me to pay attention to Grace's story while I was worrying about Rattler being in our house. But she didn't seem to notice that I was distracted and went on babbling.

"Brewster took forever to write our names in his gradebook, so I went over to Mari to ask if she was going to buy her lunch. He threw a fit and got this car seat belt out of the closet and buckled me in my chair like a baby. How embarrassed can you get?"

It'd be embarrassing, all right. "And your mom's getting you out of Brewster's room tomorrow?"

"She didn't exactly agree to that. She said if he didn't give her a satisfactory explanation, she would, though."

"What's satisfactory?" I asked.

"Something better than getting out of my seat one time."

"Maybe he was making an example of you."

"Fat chance he'll get to do that again." She looked down through the branches. "Whose car's in front of your house?"

4

"It belongs to one of my dad's friends. A guy named Rattler. They're inside drinking beer."

"Was he one of the men who stole cars with your dad so they could sell the pieces?"

"He was *the* man," I told her. "And it isn't pieces. It's parts. They parted out cars."

"I bet you hate him."

I twirled the Pepsi can around the floor while I thought that over. "I don't hate him," I said slowly. "He was always nice to me. He was like an uncle when I was a kid."

"You were a kid?" Grace's grin showed her pretty, white teeth.

"Well," I explained self-consciously, "I was only nine."

"Gracie! Gracie! Come and set the table!" Mrs. Elliott's screech cut through the tree branches from the house next door.

"Your mom should sell fish at the Pike Place market," I said.

Grace giggled and rose to her feet. "I gotta go. Did your dad get fired from his job?"

"Who knows."

After Grace left, I stayed up in the tree house awhile, wondering if my dad did get canned. Wondering what my mom would say if he did.

I found out after I'd gone to bed that night. I was drifting off to sleep when I was startled by Mom's sneezes. She must have come into the bathroom to get a Kleenex.

My mom's allergic to cigarettes, and I thought, Oh, oh, the ashtray. Dad must have flashed on the same

5

thing because I heard him say, "I'll get these butts out of here."

She was back in the living room by then and said, "Wait a minute. You don't smoke filters."

I pulled the covers around my ears. I didn't think I wanted to hear any more of this. The covers muffled the sound of Dad's voice, but not my mother's sharp questions.

"Why didn't you just explain to him that you couldn't ask him in because you didn't want to violate the conditions of your parole?" And "How long was he here?" And "How come you were home this afternoon?"

I eased my covers down. This part interested me. The walls are thin in our old house, but Dad must have been sitting over by the TV because I had to lie very quiet to catch his answer.

It was a long explanation about how another mechanic was using the air gun and Dad asked him to tighten the lug nuts on a customer's tires while Dad went to write up the customer's bill. When he gave the customer the bill, Dad figured the lugs were tightened. Only they weren't because the other mechanic forgot.

The customer came back to the tire store two hours later, hopping mad because his wheel came off on the freeway. He said he was going to sue the store and the manager blamed Dad because he'd put the tires on the man's car. Then Dad told the manager to shove his job and walked out.

Mom's voice was cold after Dad finished his story. "If I'd quit every time I got blamed for a cook's mis-

6

take, Jerry and I would have starved while you were in Monroe."

Dad told her she was making too big a deal out of the whole thing. He'd get another job.

"But when?" Mom asked.

Just as soon as he could. What more did she expect? he wanted to know.

"I expect a man for a husband," she said. "I already have one boy."

Whoa. I knew I didn't want to hear any more. Mom sounded like my grandmother, who hated Dad. I pulled the covers back over my head, put my pillow on top of them, and forced myself to sleep.

2

Purple Hair

Dad got up and had breakfast with me the next morning. "I think I'd better get out early and look for a job," he confided. "Lily found out about Rattler being here."

"I know," I said. "I heard."

He frowned into his coffee cup. "It's kinda hard to turn away an old buddy. Especially Rattler."

"But you don't want to get sent back up." I kept my attention on the toast I was buttering. I was hoping to sound casual while I tried to get the idea planted in his head.

"You're right. I don't." He took the piece of toast I handed to him. "It's funny, though. When you're on the inside, the outside seems so free. Then when you get on the outs, it's the same old hassles."

"Aren't Mom and I worth it?"

"Oh. Oh, of course. I didn't mean that." He reached over and squeezed my arm. "You're my son. You're everything I ever wanted in a boy."

"I'm not that great." This whole conversation was depressing.

9

"Yes, you are. Wait until you see the jerks running businesses out there." He slurped up the last of his coffee, gave me a good-bye pat on my back, and took off to find a job.

I finished my cereal and toast slowly. Grace banged on the front door to hurry me up. She rattled on about her jerky teacher all the way to the bus stop. Boring, but it's listen to her or nobody, since she's the only kid my age in the neighborhood.

When we got on the bus, she sat in the back with her girlfriends. I sat down next to the little kid with big glasses. There was a chorus of squeals from the back of the bus as the driver pulled into Silver King Elementary. "Look at Clayton! Look at Clayton! He dyed his hair *purple.*"

Purple? I leaned over to the window, searching for Clayton in the line of students pouring out of the bus in front of us.

The little kid scrunched back in his seat to get out of my way. When I couldn't find Clayton, the kid sighed, lifted his hand, and turned my chin toward the school entrance. "Right there," he told me.

Oh. Clayton was surrounded by a mass of kids all trying to run their fingers through his hair. "It is purple!" I blurted.

"So you're not color-blind." The little kid said it like he thought I wasn't very bright.

As soon as we were off our bus, Grace and her friends ran up to Clayton. "How did you do it?" "What did you use?" "Has your mom seen you?" "Has Mrs. Nettle seen you yet?" "What's Brewster going to say?"

While I listened to the girls' questions, I was wondering about Brewster too. Clayton was in his class. And from what Grace had told me, I figured Clayton was asking for it. Clayton didn't answer any questions, though. He just stood there with a small, one-sided smile on his face.

I didn't know Clayton very well. I'd seen him around the library and on the playground. He read a lot and kids liked him. He was kind of a mixture of a loner and a leader.

I never talked about myself or my family either, but I wished I could. I figured if anybody besides Grace found out about my dad being an ex-convict, I'd be dead in this school. Clayton seemed to keep his mouth shut because he was busy thinking. Not because he had a bad secret.

The last bell rang. The kids in Grace's class followed Clayton into their room. I followed Pete into our room across the hall. As we stashed our lunch bags on the shelf above the coat hangers, Pete said, "Purple hair looks kind of fem on a guy."

I shrugged. I wouldn't want purple hair, but I thought it was a rad thing for Clayton to do. I didn't think he'd worry about looking like a girl.

Our teacher, Mrs. McManus, is a dumpy little lady with messy red hair. She stood in front of the room waiting for us to come to order. She didn't hassle us about behaving. She just expected us to pay attention, so we did.

"Thank you," she said, after we were all quiet in our seats. She took roll and then told us that three times a week we'd have PE the last hour of the day. She said

11

the PE teacher was new to the school, his name was
Mr. Tada, and he had a black belt in karate.

"Whoa," Wayne said. "I'll be good. I'll be good. I
promise."

The whole room laughed. Mrs. McManus laughed
too.

I wondered all day what Mr. Tada was going to be
like. He was a surprise. He had a low voice, which
turned even lower when he criticized you. So low, you
were the only one who could hear him. But when he
complimented you, everybody heard him.

The gym floor is mapped out for games. About every four feet there's a yellow square. Mr. Tada started
the class by having each of us sit on a square. He said
we'd be doing gymnastics for a month and today we
were going to work on the mini-trampoline.

He said we were to remember not to land on our
stomachs because that put too much stress on
our spinal cords. He told us to leave our shoes on so
our feet wouldn't get ripped on the trampoline
springs. Then he illustrated our first exercise.

He ran light as a feather toward the trampoline,
jumped in the middle of it, sprang up high in the air,
and landed, feet together, on the blue mat. Easy, I
thought. No problem.

After we did our warm-up exercises, we lined up in
front of the trampoline. Eric, the first kid, ran toward
it, hesitated, jumped on the springs, went up about
five inches, and dumped over onto the mat.

The next three girls didn't do much better. When it
was my turn, I ran toward the trampoline, bounced in

the middle of it, and did a four-point landing on my hands and knees. Rats.

Each time I was ready for my turn, I was sure I could run light as a feather and end up on my feet. Each time I hit the mat, my knees or butt came down first. "Try to land on your two feet with your arms up," Mr. Tada whispered to me.

I was trying. I was trying.

We all tried for a half hour. Finally, Wayne, then Kate, then I got the hang of it. "You guys are doing pretty good," Mr. Tada said. "Now let's try a three-sixty."

Three-sixty? I didn't have any idea what that was. We watched as Mr. Tada ran light as a feather, jumped on the trampoline, sprang high in the air, spun like a top, and came down on his feet. Oh. He meant do a three hundred and sixty degree turn.

"When you do a three-sixty, where should your head be?" he asked us.

"It should be up," Kate answered.

"If your head is down where will you go?" Mr. Tada pointed to me.

"On your head," I said.

"That's right. Remember to keep your head straight up."

I remembered, but it isn't easy to twirl three hundred and sixty degrees in the air. Most of us splatted onto the mat after we'd done a half circle. Mr. Tada complimented us anyway.

"You guys did very well for a first time. The more you practice, the better you'll get." He had us sitting down on the yellow squares again and he was walking

13

back and forth in front of us. He wasn't much taller than Rattler. But if Rattler thought he had biceps, he should see Mr. Tada's.

Where Rattler's skinny, Mr. Tada is thick, thick with hard, flat muscles. "I've been thinking," Mr. Tada went on, "that you could get more practice if I opened the gym after school on Wednesday. At least the walkers and the bus riders who can get a ride home could stay."

I looked over at Pete. Pete nodded. His mother doesn't work and usually picks him up after a party or a game.

"How many of you would like to do gymnastics after school on Wednesdays?" Mr. Tada's black eyes swiveled left and right as he counted our raised hands. "Thirteen. And with seven from the other sixth grade, that makes twenty students. A nice group. We'll start next Wednesday after school."

Aw right! Pete and I smacked our hands together when we got up to leave the gym. This was going to be neat.

I was still thinking about trampoline practice after I left the bus with Grace. I ran a few steps ahead of her and tried to jump into a three-sixty from the sidewalk. I managed to go up about twelve inches, twirl ninety degrees, slam onto my back, and smack my head on the cement.

Grace helped me up. "What's with you anyway?" she asked.

The blow reverberated in my head. It was a few seconds before I could focus my eyes. "I was practicing a three-sixty. Doesn't your class have gym?"

14

"We have it first thing in the morning."

"First thing? That means you'll be pitted out all day."

"I know," Grace said. "Brewster's so dumb."

"Your mom come to school?"

"Yes, but I don't know what happened. She better get me out of there." Grace had started chewing on her thumbnail. She glanced at me sideways. "I suppose you're going to do gymnastics after school."

"Sure," I said. "Aren't you?"

"I don't know. I'm supposed to turn out for the church choir on Wednesdays."

I walked along beside her, rubbing the bump on my head. I didn't remember hearing her sing. "Do you sing good?"

"I sing terrible."

We had reached her house by then. I was about to say I'd see her later, when I remembered Clayton's purple hair. "What did Brewster do about Clayton's dye job?"

"He said that it was 'disturbing the educational process of the classroom' and Clayton would have to get out."

"Get out to where?"

"To the office to call his mother to come get him."

"That Brewster's unbelievable."

"Tell me about it."

"Do you want to come over and shoot a few baskets after you change?"

She looked toward the back of her house, where we could see her brother, Matt, and her mom raking leaves. "I will if I don't have to help clean up the yard."

15

I nodded and split for my house. As I went up the steps, I held my breath. There weren't any cars in front, so Rattler shouldn't be inside. I was hoping my dad wasn't either.

I turned the doorknob slowly. The living room was empty. Good. That meant Dad was still looking for a job or had one. Which also meant that he wouldn't have time for his old buddies. I whistled a Van Halen guitar break as I headed for the fridge to see what Mom had left for a snack.

3

Wiseguys

I was up in my tree house chomping on an apple and trying to finish a story in my reading book when a mass argument started next door. Grace must have gotten trapped into the leaf raking. It sounded like she'd been aced out of gymnastics too.

I put down my book and eased silently around the platform until I had a good view of the action. Matt was stuffing leaves into a trash bag, Mrs. Elliott had her gloved hands planted on her hips, and Grace was whacking a rake into the ground. "Stupid, stupid, stupid!"

"Are you calling me stupid?" Mrs. Elliott reminded me of a cartoon traffic cop as she shook her big white garden glove at Grace.

"No, I'm not calling you stupid." Grace gave the ground another whack. "I'm calling the whole idea of me singing in a choir stupid."

Matt took a quick look at his mother. Her face was swelling with rage. "Um, Mom," he said quietly. "Grace sings about as good as those blue jays up there."

Mrs. Elliott glanced briefly at the jays squawking in the hazelnut trees. With their black crests and blue feathers, they were colored like Grace too. In fact, all of the Elliotts, except the Reverend, have black hair and blue eyes.

"Well," Mrs. Elliott said, calming down a bit, "it's time Grace took part in church activities. She can learn to sing."

"Learn to sing!" Grace jerked her rake up and down. "Sure I can, Mom. That's why the singing teacher tells me to shut up so I won't knock all the other kids off key."

"She better not tell you to shut up. I better not hear about her saying anything like that."

"So, she told me to sing softly so I wouldn't sway the other kids out of tune. And what are you going to do? Get me out of her class like you're getting me out of Brewster's?"

"I never said I would get you out of Mr. Brewster's class. I said I agreed with Mrs. Nettle that first he should have a chance to get used to teaching. After all, this is his first year and he spent twenty-five years in the army."

The army part must have struck Matt funny because he heaved the trash bag over his shoulder and marched into the garage humming a military tune. Mrs. Elliott watched him with pursed lips before turning back to Grace. "Next Wednesday you'll start in the choir without any more arguing. And will you please pay attention to what you're doing. You're supposed to be cleaning the yard, not ruining the lawn."

Grace flipped the wooden handle toward her mom.

18

"You know how to sing and you know how to rake, so you go ahead and do it." Grace took off for the back door.

Mrs. Elliott opened her mouth. Then closed it as Grace disappeared. I imagined Grace stamping up the steps inside her house. After that her bedroom door slammed. Her room's eye-level with my tree house and I not only heard her window crack, I saw her shoe hit it.

Mrs. Elliott's mouth was wide open again. "Gracie!" she screamed.

When Mrs. Elliott reached Grace's room, there was a lot more yelling. Even though I was fifteen feet away and the cracked window was closed, their screeches pierced the air. I guess Matt heard them, too, because I saw him hurry out of the garage and take off toward his dad's church.

I had eaten the last bite out of my apple and tossed the core to the ground, when Reverend Elliott came across his backyard with Matt following him. I couldn't see them go in their back door, but I heard it open and close. I kept my eyes on Grace's window. I only saw shadows through the glass, though.

The screeching stopped and the low rumbling of Reverend Elliott's voice drifted across to my tree house. And soon even that ended. I tried to go back to my homework, but I kept thinking that since Grace's mom is missing a few screws, it's lucky that the Reverend's a cool head. He saved my butt last year after I beat up a kid who'd found out about my dad and tried to blackmail me. It's handy to have a guy like that around.

19

* * *

I didn't find out what happened to Grace until the next morning. She was quiet when she joined me on the way to the bus stop. Her face was puffy and her eyelids were rimmed with pink. "You been crying?" I asked.

"What do you think?" she snapped.

I shrugged. "I guess you're not going to the tumbling class."

"No. And even if I get kicked out of the choir, I don't get to go."

"How can you get kicked out of a church choir?"

"Oh, they don't actually kick you out. You stand there with a big red face while the choirmaster suggests that you might be happier doing something else. I'm going to last about half an hour."

I saw the bus coming down the street so I put my hand on Grace's back to hurry her along. As we waited for the bus to pull up to the curb, I asked, "But why can't you go to Tada's class after that?"

"Because," she said, "I broke my window and was disrespectful to my mom and until I can learn to be respectful she isn't going to do anything for me like picking me up after school."

"Maybe she'll let you ride with Pete's mom," I suggested.

"Not a chance," she said, and went for the open doors of the bus.

Bummer, I thought to myself before I climbed up the bus steps after her.

It turned out that I might as well have kept my sympathy for myself. By the time the weekend was

20

over my family was in more trouble than Grace's could ever imagine. The first feeling of dread came over me at dinner that night.

Dad'd heated up frozen dishes of macaroni and cheese. When I'd porked half of mine down, I noticed he was just stirring his food around on his foil tray.

"Um, how was job hunting today?" I asked him.

"Nowhere," he said.

"Nothing in the paper either?"

"Sure," he said, "I can work in any hamburger joint for four-fifty an hour. That should keep me in cigarettes and bus fare."

My dad is never a bitter guy. At least not in front of me. I sat across the kitchen table from him trying to figure out a way to make him feel better. It wouldn't help to suggest that he should have kept his mouth shut on his last job. He'd been getting paid nine dollars an hour in the tire store.

The only thing I could think of to say was "Maybe there'll be some good openings in Sunday's want ads. The paper'll come out tomorrow afternoon."

"Maybe." He pushed back his chair and lit a cigarette. I finished my macaroni and cheese while he smoked.

"How about we have some ice cream for dessert," I suggested.

"You have some. I think I'll go for a walk." He ground out his butt in the ashtray. "You know, Son, it isn't so easy to get a job when the only reference you have is the warden. Remember that."

You remember it, I wanted to tell him.

He went for his walk and I worried, but he was back

21

before Mom came home. She'd brought him a six-pack. He drank up two of the cans while watching TV, still not saying much.

After I'd gone to bed, I heard her ask him how the job hunting had gone.

"Nowhere," he said.

The next afternoon he drove Mom to work so he could use her car. He was home again about five o'clock, carrying a rumpled Saturday edition of the Sunday paper. I came out of my room to ask him, "How'd it go?"

"It didn't," he said.

At dinner I tried to make him laugh by describing Clayton's purple hair. The story got one little smile.

He had on a big smile a half hour later, though. That's when Rattler banged on our front door and brought in a sleazy-looking friend. Rattler slapped Dad on the back. "Have Louis and I got a hot deal for you!"

Then he saw me coming in from the kitchen. "And here's the number-one son, Jerry Junior."

I mumbled hello while my stomach tightened over my dinner. What lousy timing. The last thing Dad needed was to have his job problem solved by Rattler and Louis's hot deal.

"I got something for you too," Rattler said to me, pulling out his wallet. "How about a ten-spot to take a friend to the movies?"

I looked up at Dad for help. I didn't get any. "You could treat that blue-eyed girl next door," he said.

I stood there. Rattler poked the bill at me. I knew

this was a bribe to get rid of me, but I couldn't think of a way to refuse it.

Rattler tucked the ten dollars in the pocket of my jeans, gave me a pat on my shoulder, and said, "Have yourself a time, kid."

I gave him what I knew was a sickly grin and went for my bedroom. I left my door open two inches and stood behind it without moving a muscle, hoping to hear what was up.

I caught the words *Alderwood Mall . . . that parking lot will be crammed full. . . . Louis here can open a can in half a second. . . .*

Then silence. Footsteps. I tried to get out from behind my door, but it banged in my face. "Hey," Dad said, "I thought you were going to the movies."

I closed the door with one hand and rubbed my nose with the other. "Dad, can we talk about this, please?"

"Later. Later. We'll talk later. I need to talk to Rattler now." He must have seen the panic on my face, because he ruffled my hair. "You worry too much. Go out and have yourself a good time."

Before I could think of the words *parole violation* and *ex-felons,* Dad was back in the living room. There was nothing for me to do but take off. I got my jacket, left the house through the kitchen, hesitated at the edge of Grace's yard. Then I climbed up into my tree house.

Hunkered down behind the fir tree limbs, I tried desperately to think of a way to stop what I knew was going to happen.

4

The Big Jump

Grace climbed up the ladder to the tree house and sat down beside me on the platform. I turned to look at her. "Your mom isn't mad at you anymore?"

"She's still mad," Grace replied, "but she's gone shopping at the mall because there's a white sale."

"So, it's true." I felt like I was going to puke.

"What's true?" She peered into my face. "You look awful. You sick or something?"

"I'm sick all right. And getting sicker."

"What's the matter with you?"

"Nothing's the matter with me. It's my dad. He's going to get himself sent back up."

"How's he going to manage that?"

"Easy. He and his friends are going to hot-wire some cars at the mall."

Grace's eyes widened. "And steal them, you mean?"

"You got it," I said.

"That's rough."

"That's real rough. It's my dad. It's real rough."

Grace and I have been friends for a year. We never touch each other or anything, but I felt that she wanted to reach out a hand to me now. Instead, she twisted her fingers around in her lap. "Couldn't you talk to your dad?"

"I tried. He's too busy talking to his friends. They're in the house planning their job. As soon as they come out, they'll head for the mall."

This kind of stuff is like a storybook to Grace. She wrinkled her face in thought. "Are you sure? Maybe they're planning it for tomorrow. Maybe you can talk your dad out of it after his friends leave."

"Is the sale on tomorrow?" I asked.

Her face was still wrinkled up. "I don't think so. I think it's one of those six o'clock to midnight things. My mom rushed out right after dinner."

"Then I've had it."

"Maybe." She looked into my face. "Maybe you could just go into your house and say you don't want your dad to get in trouble or a boy needs his dad or something."

"PK, get real. They already gave me ten bucks to get rid of me."

"Oh."

We sat together in silence. I wasn't kidding about getting sicker and sicker. Any minute Rattler and sleazy Louis and Dad would come out the front door.

Grace suddenly brightened and let out a laugh. "I know. If your dad starts to leave the house with his friends, you can pretend to fall out of the tree and I'll rush up to tell them you broke your arm and your dad will have to take you to the hospital. And that always takes forever because of the examinations and the X rays and things."

26

I thought that over. Grace is innocent, but she isn't stupid. Her idea just might work. I crawled to the edge of the platform and looked down. It was at least fifteen feet to the ground.

"Wait a minute." Grace crawled up next to me. "I mean pretend. Not really do it."

"I'd have to really do it. Those guys con people all the time. They aren't going to believe some phony moans."

Grace was chewing on her thumbnail again. "Can't you jump from the ladder? That'll scare me enough to make me scream."

"Naw, I'd just end up below the ladder and that wouldn't look like I broke an arm." I leaned out farther to inspect the tree's lower branches. "I might be able to swing from that big limb there and then drop the rest of the way."

"That's scary. What if the limb broke?"

It was scary. I pulled back from the edge of the platform. So did Grace.

"I can't think of anything else that would stop my dad. Can you?" I asked her.

"No. He sure is a weird dad. Every time I see him he seems so friendly."

"He is friendly," I said. "But there's something the matter with him. He does things without ever figuring out the consequences."

"I wonder what the consequences of your jump are going to be."

I turned up both my hands. "What other choice do I have?"

We sat there, Grace chewing on her thumbnail and

27

me wondering if I'd really have the guts to jump fifteen feet.

"I hear something," Grace said.

Together, we pulled the tree branches apart for a
view of my front porch. First there was Louis, then
Rattler, then Dad.

I hitched myself closer to the platform's edge.
"They're going to do it."

"Wait. Wait." Grace took ahold of my arm. "Maybe
your dad's just saying good-bye."

He wasn't saying good-bye. He was walking right
down the steps with the other guys. I shook Grace's
hand off.

"Oh, no. Oh, no," she whispered.

I crept the rest of the way on my hands and knees,
took a lumpy swallow, reached out for the big limb,
and fell forward. The limb cracked under my weight,
something pulled loose in my arm, and a burning pain
shot through my shoulder. I let go, saw a flash of the
ground, and put a hand out to stop my fall. My wrist
crumpled under me as I hit the dirt.

I heard Grace screaming. I couldn't get air into my
lungs. My wrist and shoulder hurt so bad, I thought I
was going to faint. Grace was screaming and screaming and I couldn't breathe.

Dad's face was above me. "My God, what happened?"

"He's got the wind knocked out of him," I heard
Rattler say.

Dad kneeled behind me, put his arms around my
chest, and squeezed. I guess he didn't know what else
to do.

28

"You'd better be careful," I heard Louis warn. "His back might be injured."

I tried to breathe, but my throat was locked. No sound came out of my mouth. I could hear voices, but I couldn't hear words anymore. I could only feel pain and fear.

Dad squeezed again.

My chest jerked with short coughs, letting in bits of air. I slipped out of Dad's arms and lay on the ground gasping and hurting.

"Can you move your legs?" Dad asked.

I moved my legs. "It's my shoulder and wrist."

"Let's get him to the hospital," Rattler said.

Dad picked me up and carried me to the car. Rattler helped ease me into the front seat. Then he and Louis got in back. I remember seeing Grace through the window as we drove off. She was standing on the curb. Worry covered her face as she ripped at her thumbnail with her teeth.

The hospital was just as Grace predicted. Slow. First we saw a nurse. Then we waited. Then we saw the doctor. I bloodied my lip trying not to cry out when he poked around my shoulder. "Well, let's get some X rays before we do anything else," he said.

The nurse put a heavy vest on my chest before she carefully placed my arm on the flat white tray and lowered the nose of the X-ray machine. "Now just hold that position for a minute," she said. My wrist and shoulder ached so bad, my mouth hung open while I followed her directions like a robot.

Dad and Rattler were in the hall when I came out of

29

the X-ray room. Dad was saying, "I know, but I'll have to stay with my boy. You go ahead and take the keys."

When he saw me, he tossed the car keys to Rattler as if it were no big thing. I hurt too much to care what happened to Rattler and Louis. I sat down on one of the hall chairs and waited with my mouth open and my eyes closed.

A different nurse came and put us in another little room. A while later the doctor came with a cheery face and said, "It's just what I thought, a dislocated shoulder."

After he had me stretch out on the examining table, he put one hand on my chest and took my arm with the other hand. He pulled my arm over my head, around to the side, and then gave it a massive yank. I screamed.

Dad's white face was bent over me as I felt my arm slip back into its socket. "Now you should feel better," the doctor said. I lay on the table panting. Gradually, gradually the piercing pain eased into a dull ache.

"There's no fracture, but you've sprained that wrist." The doctor was over at a wall cabinet taking out a tan bandage. "I'll wrap it for you. Keep it wrapped except when you shower. Have your family doctor look at it in two weeks."

"He'll be okay until then?" Dad asked.

"Oh, he's going to feel pretty uncomfortable for a few days. Luckily, the sprain's on his left wrist so he'll be able to do his schoolwork as soon as the soreness leaves his right shoulder. He should skip any physical exercise though. No bike riding, swimming, or ball playing."

30

I turned my head to watch the doctor wrap the bandage around and around my wrist. "How about tumbling?"

That made him laugh. "I think you've done enough tumbling for a while."

Out in the reception room, I stayed beside Dad while a clerk totaled our bill on a computer. No tumbling for two weeks! Gymnastics only lasted a month.

"Let's see if Rattler's back with our car," Dad said. "Or would you rather sit in a chair while I look?"

"You can look," I told him. I didn't feel much like walking around a parking lot.

I sat down in a chair and did nothing. I would've liked to flip through the stack of magazines on the table, but my wrist throbbed and my shoulder ached. It hurt the least when I kept both arms still.

About fifteen minutes went by before Dad came back in. He paced around the room, took out a cigarette, saw the NO SMOKING sign, and tossed the cigarette in a wastebasket. After about five minutes, he went back to see if Rattler had arrived. He hadn't.

Dad went out and came in and went out and came in. I watched the clock on the hospital wall. When it was five to ten, I suggested he call Mom because she'd be expecting him to pick her up.

"Ya, right," he agreed. "Maybe she can find a ride at the restaurant and pick us up."

She could. And she did. When she arrived, she was so full of questions about my accident that she didn't ask about the car until her friend dropped us off at our house. Dad didn't answer her right away.

31

"Let's get Jerry to bed," he said. "He's had a rough night."

That suited me fine. I didn't want to be around when Mom found out that Rattler had taken her car. I heard rumblings from the living room anyway, then Dad yelling, "What's the big deal about lending your car to a couple friends?" And Mom screaming, "Don't try to give me that same old crap. Promises mean nothing to you. You're never going to change!"

The front door slammed, and a while later I heard Mom's bedroom door close. Then Dad coming back in the front door. No footsteps toward their bedroom, though. Just silence. I figured he'd crashed on the couch the way he usually did when they'd had a fight.

It took a long time for me to go to sleep. Partly because I was depressed about what Mom had screamed, and partly because my shoulder and wrist ached. Most nights I curled up on my side, but that made my shoulder hurt worse. The best position was on my back with both arms stretched out flat. Only I wasn't used to sleeping that way and I kept wanting to turn over.

It was just getting light when I was awakened by a loud knocking. I lay quiet, trying to figure out who could be knocking so early Sunday morning. Then I remembered. It could be Rattler. It could be the police.

I eased myself up and over to my bedroom door. I opened it a few inches before climbing back into bed. That's when I heard Dad's voice from the living room. "Yes? What is it?"

32

A deep voice. "We'd like to speak to Lily Johnson, please."

Cops. It had to be the cops.

I lay shivering as Mom's footsteps came from her bedroom.

"What's the matter?" I heard Mom say.

"Do you own a 1980 Camaro?" the cop asked.

"Yes, I do," she said.

"Where is it?"

"It should be in the garage," Dad said, using his innocent voice. "Oh, no, I remember. Some friends borrowed it."

The cop wasn't here for casual conversation. His voice was dead serious. "And you are?"

"Gerald Johnson."

"Did you lend the car to your friends?"

"Yes," Dad admitted.

"We'd like you to come with us to answer a few questions about your friends."

"Certainly," Dad said.

My heart thumped in my chest while I listened to footsteps going down our front steps. The sound of a car motor slowly faded as I imagined the police car drawing away from the curb and disappearing down the street. The cops would be in the front seat and my dad would be in the back behind the metal grille.

5

Don't Pass
the Oysters

Mom was in the living room sitting in the big chair with her feet propped on the footstool. She was wearing her flowered kimono and slippers. Where the kimono fell away from her legs, I could see her white skin mapped with bulging purple lines. The flat-heeled sandals hadn't cured her varicose veins, and it was lucky she never found out I stole them.

The Sunday paper was on the floor beside her where Dad had left it. She was just sitting there. Not reading it or anything. I reached out my hand. "How about passing me the funnies?"

"No," she said. "I want to talk to you."

I backed up to the couch and sat down on the edge, waiting.

She stared across the room at me. "Who's got the car?"

"You mean your car?"

"Don't pull that," she told me. "I mean the car. Where is it? Who's got it?"

"I don't know where it is." I rubbed my wrist, hoping to get her sympathy. It didn't work.

"Gerald! *Who has the car? Who had the car last night?*"

"I think maybe one of Dad's friends took it."

"He told me that much. I'm asking you for their names."

"Rattler."

"And who else?"

"Well, I don't know if . . ."

"Your father said *friends*, not *friend*. Now, who else?"

It was no use making her mad at me for nothing because she'd find out anyway. "I don't know the guy."

"What'd he look like?"

"Um." I didn't want to say sleazy, so I said, "He was wearing a gray suit. It fit kinda tight. He had yellowish hair slicked back . . ."

"And his name was Louis." Her mouth had tightened into a straight line.

I rubbed my wrist some more. It was really aching now. My guts were curdled from worrying, and Mom was making me feel worse. She just sat there with her lips held tight against her clenched teeth.

"When do you think Dad will be coming back?"

"He may not be coming back."

"But why? He didn't do anything. He was at the hospital with me."

"Were Rattler and Louis at the hospital too?"

"Um. Ya, they helped Dad get me in the car."

"And after you got to the hospital they took the car?"

"Yes, but Dad didn't go anywhere with them."

She squinted her eyes as if she were looking inside

36

at her thoughts. I had the uneasy feeling that she would like to dump Dad.

"He should be able to come home because he didn't do anything," I said.

"Oh, yes, he did. He broke his parole. One of the rules of his parole was that he couldn't associate with ex-felons. That means men who have served time in prison. Which both Rattler and Louis have done."

"But it's kind of hard for Dad to turn away a buddy when he comes to the door."

She let out a bitter laugh. "You bet it is."

"Maybe the police will think Dad just lent his old friends the car and didn't really associate with them. Maybe they'll think he didn't even let them in the door."

Mom heaved herself out of the chair. "I'm afraid you're going to have to grow up, Jerry. Police check out stories. And they'll check out the hospital."

I stood up too. "So that means he'll have to go back to the reformatory?"

She gave my back a pat and her voice softened a bit. "It will depend on the parole officer and the prosecutor. They'll decide. It's no use your worrying about it. Come on. Let's get some breakfast."

I followed her into the kitchen, knowing I wasn't going to be able to eat, knowing there was no way I could stop worrying about my dad.

Climbing a ladder with a sore shoulder and sprained wrist isn't the easiest thing to do, but I wanted to be by myself in the tree house. After breakfast I'd waited three hours for Dad to call or to come home. Mom sat in her chair the whole time, saying nothing, and I pretended to read the funnies.

Finally, Mom said she guessed they'd be holding Dad overnight. She was going to walk to the grocery store and did I want to come. I didn't.

I crouched against the tree trunk, rubbing my wrist and hurting inside and out. Dad had promised Mom that things were going to be different. He'd promised on the North Star that we'd both go straight. I knew he loved me and Mom, so why wouldn't he be careful about what he did? If you loved your family, wouldn't you keep your promises? That's the part that hurt me most.

I could hear Grace's brother, Matt, washing his car in the driveway below. Besides the sound of running water, I kept hearing a buzzing. Then my eyes focused on a hornet that was zipping up and down along the edge of the tree house. And then there was another one. And another one. I leaned forward to get a closer look. They were big suckers. Striped yellow and black. I bet they had big stingers in their rear ends too. I decided my tree house wasn't such a neat place to be after all.

I eased down the ladder, using mostly my right hand with the bum shoulder. When I got to the ground, Matt called out to me. "See you got some new tenants."

"What?" I yelled back.

"Some company." He squirted his hose toward my tree house.

I pulled the lower branches apart and looked up. There it was, a gray globe hanging under the platform.

38

Hornets were crawling in and out a hole in the bottom of the nest. Whoa!

I let go of the branches and walked over to the bushes that divided our yards. "How do you get rid of that thing?"

Matt grinned at me. "You can knock it down with rocks."

"No way," I told him. "I'd get stung."

"Probably." He was grinning all over now. He dropped the hose on the ground and began wiping his black car with a rag. He keeps that car shining like a mirror.

I let out a long sigh. "Guess that's the end of my tree house."

"Wait a minute," he said. "I'll get the nest down for you." He picked up the hose and headed through the bushes to the fir tree.

I followed six feet behind him. "What are you going to do? Those hornets will sting you too."

"Not a chance. And they're not hornets. They're paper wasps."

They looked like hornets to me. I watched as Matt positioned himself in an opening between two branches, raised his hose, turned the nozzle on full blast, and pointed it at the nest.

I backed up another three feet as the wasps streamed out of their entrance and flew frantically around the water. Slowly the gray paper globe became sopping wet and plopped to the ground with the wasps flying after it.

"Wow, you did it!" I told Matt.

"Stay away," he ordered. "Wait for them to give

up." He swished the water back and forth, soaking the wasps until they made a beeline out of the yard or dropped into the puddle beside the nest.

"What's going on?" Grace had come up beside me and poked me in the right shoulder.

"Take it easy," I said. "It still hurts."

"Oh, I'm sorry. Is your wrist broken?"

"No, it's only sprained."

Matt backed up to us. "What happened to you, anyway?"

"I jumped out of the tree house," I said.

He frowned. "Maybe you kids shouldn't be playing up there."

"Oh, it's safe," Grace said quickly. "I just kind of dared Jerry to swing down from a limb."

He turned his frown on her. "That was dumb."

"I know," she agreed. "Jerry had to go to the hospital."

"Thanks a lot for getting rid of the wasps' nest," I said.

"Sure." Matt dragged his hose through the bushes and back to his car.

"Don't ever tell him anything," Grace whispered to me. "He thinks he's my second father."

"I think he's pretty neat."

"Sometimes. Listen, what about your dad? Did it all come out okay?"

I shook my head. "No, something went wrong. The cops found Mom's car and maybe they have Rattler and they took my dad away this morning."

She started to touch my shoulder and then must

40

have remembered it was sore. She gave me a little smile instead. "I'm sorry."

I shrugged. "That's the breaks, I guess."

"Yes, but—"

"Gracie! Matt!" Mrs. Elliott was at their front door screeching. "It's time to go."

"We're going to my grandma's," Grace explained. "I'll see you tomorrow on the way to school."

She went home and I went in my house to sit by the phone and worry some more.

Mom came in the front door juggling two grocery sacks. "I got oysters for your dinner," she told me.

"Thanks." Oysters? In my sick stomach?

"Your dad didn't call?" she asked.

"No."

I set the table while she fried the oysters. It was a bit like old times when Dad had been in the reformatory. But those were times of hopeful waiting.

Mom watched me clumsily cut the oysters in small pieces so I could get them down. "You don't have to eat if you don't feel like it."

"I don't much." I pushed the plate away.

She looked at me with even sadder eyes than Grace had. "I know how much you love him. And how hard this is."

She shouldn't have said that. I knocked the chair over, leaving the table. I was too old for her to see me cry.

In the bathroom, I washed my face in cold water over and over again. She was in the living room when I came out and sat down on the couch.

41

"Jerry," she said, shuffling the Sunday paper into a neat pile on her lap. "When your wrist is better, I want you to take down the tree house."

"No."

"Yes. It's obviously too dangerous. Next time you fall out you could break your arm. Or Grace could, and we don't have insurance."

"I didn't fall," I said. "You'd have to be stupid to fall out of there."

"Your dad said you fell."

"That's what I told him, but I really jumped."

"You jumped!" She leaned her head toward me with her eyebrows scrunched together. "But why?"

"So Dad wouldn't go off with Rattler," I said softly.

She leaned even farther toward me. "What?"

"So Dad would have to take care of me and couldn't go off with Rattler." I said it really loud this time.

She stared at me as if she couldn't understand my words, and then she dropped her head and covered her eyes with her hands. Slowly the tears seeped out between her fingers and splotched the paper in her lap.

6

Back in the Slammer

Mom thought it'd take at least a week for the prosecutor and parole officer to make a decision about Dad. By Thursday I was going nuts at school trying to sit still in my seat. Especially during the math time tests. Mrs. McManus is big on time tests.

She sent me along with the rest of the kids to the gym. Mom had written a note to excuse me from PE, but Mrs. McManus said I'd probably like watching the class better than reading in the library again.

PE began with with push-ups, head rolls, and shoulder shrugs. Sitting against the wall by myself, I tried the shoulder shrugs. I could do them okay. It was my left wrist that I couldn't use.

Mr. Tada lined up the kids to show them how to slam-dunk the basketball while bouncing off the trampoline. It nearly killed me to be left out. No one in the class even got the ball near the basket. I would have been the best in the room.

When Mr. Tada started the kids on the balance beam, I'd had it. "I can do that," I told him, getting up from my place by the wall. "It's only my wrist that's sore."

He squinted his black eyes with concern. "Are you sure?"

"Sure I'm sure." I lined up behind Pete and did the dip step on the beam with the rest of the kids. Somehow my wrist made me teeter, but at least the hour went fast.

On the walk home from the bus, I alternated between spurting ahead of Grace and walking backward to let her catch up. "What's with you anyway?" she complained.

"I wanna see if there's a message about Dad."

"Oh," she said. "I think your mom's car is in front of your house."

Without even saying "See ya" to Grace, I whirled around and zipped the rest of the way home. Nobody was in the living room. I found Mom in the kitchen making a cup of coffee. "You heard from Dad?" I asked her.

"Yes," she said slowly. "Come and sit on the couch with me."

It was bad news, for sure. I followed her out of the kitchen, sat down beside her, and barely breathed while she placed her cup on the coffee table.

"I'm sorry, honey, but they're sending him up for ninety days for violating his parole." She reached out and smoothed the hair back from my face.

I pulled away from her. "Ninety days for just seeing Rattler? That's not fair."

"Louis was caught breaking into a truck at the mall.

44

Rattler was parked next to him. He had two sets of out-of-state license plates on the seat of my car."

"But Dad wasn't there."

"They didn't say he was. However, he'd obviously seen Rattler."

"Bummer. Poor Dad. The poor guy. What'd they do to Rattler?"

"I don't know." She picked up her coffee cup and took a sip.

"How'd you get your car back?"

"The police released it to me."

I thought a minute. "Why didn't you go to work after you got the car?"

"Because I wanted to have dinner with you."

It was a sad dinner. Neither of us could think of much to talk about. While she was scooping up ice cream for dessert, I did say, "He'll be out before Christmas."

"Yes," she agreed. "He will."

"It'll be fun."

She didn't agree with that, just handed me my ice cream and sat down to drink more coffee.

"Aren't you going to have some dessert?"

"No." She was staring over her coffee cup at the wall behind me. Something in the thoughtful way she'd tilted her head made me uneasy again.

"Anyway this time he'll have learned his lesson," I said.

"I doubt it." She spoke so softly, I could barely hear the words.

* * *

Grace didn't ask me about my dad the next morning. She took one look at my face and knew. I hardly talked to her on the way to the bus. And after I got on, I sat next to the little kid who always stared out the window.

When I got in the classroom, I found a strange girl at the desk in front of mine. She had short yellow hair and a small snow-sled nose that her glasses slid down. She turned to look at me after I was in my seat. It was a shy, frightened look, and when I didn't say anything she turned back around.

After Mrs. McManus took roll, she announced, "Class, we have a new student. This is Summer from Mount Vernon."

Russell, who's the dumbest kid in our room, blurted out, "Is Summer her first name or her last?"

Mrs. McManus gave him her steady stare, which made Russell remember to raise his hand. Mrs. McManus nodded.

"What's her whole name?" he asked.

"It's Summer Day. Isn't that pretty?"

Russell tried to wipe off his grin with his fingers. I watched the back of Summer's head. A thick pink blush spread from her cheeks down and around her neck. Summer Day. What a stupid name to hang on a kid.

She kept her mouth shut and her head poked over her arithmetic paper for most of the morning. When it was time to clear our desks for lunch, she turned around again. She looked so helpless, I pulled out of my funk to ask her, "Did you bring your lunch?"

She shook her head.

46

"Then you go down the hall and around the corner. There'll be some long tables where the cooks serve the food. Just follow the rest of the kids that are buying."

I was porking down my chicken sandwich and talking to Pete between bites, when she came back with her tray. Pete sits beside me and I was asking him to tell me everything that had happened in the after-school gymnastics class. I didn't want to get too far behind while my wrist healed.

Pete was saying Mr. Tada had spent most of the hour explaining the equipment, when Summer suddenly jerked in her seat and let out a loud, "Oh, no! Oh, no!" Then she clapped both hands over her face as if she were going to puke.

Mrs. McManus left her desk and hurried to Summer's side along with half the class. I pushed out of my chair and leaned over Summer's shoulder. She took her hand away from her mouth long enough to point at her half-eaten slice of pizza. There, at the edge of her teeth print, was a big black fly baked in the dough.

"That's disgusting," Linda said as she and Kate backed down the aisle.

"Gross!" Wayne said.

"You ought to sue the cooks," Robert said. His father's a lawyer and he's all for suing everybody.

"Now calm down," Mrs. McManus said. "These things can happen. Summer, take your tray to the cooks and ask for another pizza."

Summer shook her head and shrank even farther down in her seat. She still had her hands over her mouth, and I was worried that she might really puke. I grabbed her tray. "I'll get you a new lunch."

47

"No, just take it away, please." Her head was tilted up to me. I couldn't help but notice that behind her glasses her slanted eyes were sea green.

I brought back two cookies and plunked them on her desk. She inspected them carefully before nibbling on one. She did it just to be polite. From the downturn of her mouth it was obvious her stomach wasn't up to more food.

I went to the gymnastics class the next Wednesday after school. My wrist was bending easily so I unwound the bandage and left it off. I never told Mom that I was supposed to see a doctor. I'd seen her shudder after she opened the electric bill.

The class was more fun than regular PE. There were fewer kids and Mr. Tada let us choose to work on the parallel bars, trampoline, or the wedge-shaped mat called a cheese. Pete did front handsprings on the cheese. I slam-dunked from the trampoline.

When Mr. Tada was confident that Wayne could spot the kids on the bars, he came over to watch the line in front of the mini-trampoline. "You handle the ball very well," Mr. Tada told me after I'd made a perfect shot.

My insides swelled with pride, but I tried to give him a nonchalant smile. My dad had always said I had good basketball hands.

Pete's mom picked five of us up after class. She let Mari, Kate, and Eric off first. On the way to my house she turned her head toward the backseat and asked, "What does your father do, Jerry?"

"He's a mechanic."

48

"Pete said your mother's a waitress at Patrick's Grill."

"She is," I said.

"You better get on your side of the road, Mom," Pete told her.

Mrs. McCartney swerved the car over to the right, and I hoped that was the last of her questions. It wasn't.

She kept her head faced forward, but talked louder. "Where does your father work?"

I thought fast. "In Monroe."

"Oh, out there." She pulled up at a stop sign and glanced back at me again. "Are your mother and father fortunate enough to have the same hours?"

"No," I said. "My mom works the dinner shift."

"So do you make dinner at home or does your dad?"

Pete gave his mom a poke in the shoulder. "The road's clear."

She shifted into gear, and before she could think up any more questions Pete told her to turn left at the next block. My house was two more blocks down the street. I hopped out of the car as soon as we got there. "Thanks for the ride."

As I unlocked the front door I congratulated myself on not giving Pete's mother any damaging answers. Too bad that later in the night I wasn't as lucky with my mom.

49

7

The Trap

I was sound asleep when I heard my mother call my name. At first I thought I was dreaming and awoke only enough to turn over in bed. Then she shook me. Hard. I opened my eyes to see her angry face. "Get up," she said. "Get up right now."

"Is it Dad?" I asked, throwing my covers off.

"No, it isn't. It's you. And put some pants on."

Mom was sitting in her chair in the living room when I got there. Her face was stony in the lamplight. I knew she thought I'd done something terrible, but I couldn't think of what it could be. We were usually good friends. But now she looked at me as if I were a monster.

I sat down on the couch across from her. "Wh-what's up?" I asked.

She kicked the white sandals off her feet. They landed in the middle of the room. I stared down at them, my heart thumping so hard, it must have been bulging out of my chest. Somehow she'd found out I'd stolen the sandals.

"Where did you get those things?" she demanded.

"At a—at a sale in the mall. Dad sent me money for your Christmas present."

"How much money?" She barked the question out.

I was thinking as fast as I could. She knew what Dad earned in prison. There was no use lying. I didn't want to lie to her anyway. "Twenty dollars," I whispered.

"How much?" Her voice was loud.

"Twenty dollars," I repeated, wishing this were a nightmare.

"Those things are made of real snakeskin, aren't they?"

"I'm not sure. I think part of them are. The scaly side."

"Right," she said. "And real snakeskin costs a lot of money, doesn't it? One of my customers said she had seen a pair of sandals just like mine in the mall, but they were too expensive for her to buy. She said she liked snakeskin because it wears so well. I always wondered why those things never wore out. Now I know, don't I?"

I didn't answer her.

"How much did they cost?" she asked.

"I got them at a sale, remember."

"I remember. And how much did you pay for them?"

There was no use answering that question either. I just sat there. And she sat there. Finally, in a dead-level voice she said, "You stole them, didn't you?"

I took in a big breath and dared to look across the room at her. "I wanted them so your legs wouldn't hurt. So—so your veins wouldn't pop out so much."

"You wanted them." Her head was nodding up and

52

down and she was talking in that same voice that was scaring me to death. "You wanted them so you took them. Just like your father does. Whatever he wants he takes. Right?"

"No. No, Mom. No." I couldn't stand the cold way she was acting. "No. I did take them and then I was sorry. Dad and I swore on the North Star that we'd go straight and wouldn't steal again. And I haven't stolen anything since."

"Just like your father?"

"Well, he hasn't stolen . . ." My words dribbled away. I knew and she knew that he would have if he hadn't taken me to the hospital. I tried again. "Mom, listen. I didn't want to be a thief. I don't want to be a thief. I haven't done it again."

"And you're not going to. You are not going to turn out like your dad. Believe me. Now go to bed."

I didn't get off the couch. I knew she was planning something terrible. "Mom, wait. What do you mean? What are you going to do? I'm real sorry about the sandals."

"Go to bed, Jerry. Tomorrow is my day off. We'll talk about it when you get home from school."

There was nothing else for me to do but go to bed. But not to sleep, that was for sure. I tossed around and worried and swore at myself for stealing the sandals until the morning light came through my bedroom window.

Mom must have slept, though. I wasn't about to make a sound until I heard her in the kitchen. She was on the phone making an appointment when I got in

53

there. I sat at the table and waited for her to put the phone down.

After she hung up, she stood in the middle of the kitchen staring at me. "What are you doing home? Why aren't you in school?"

"I want to know what my punishment is."

Her shoulders sagged as she pulled out the chair beside me. "I'm not going to punish you, Jerry. It's just my responsibility to raise you up to be a good person."

"You don't believe I'm a good person?"

"Yes, I believe you're a good person now, love. But I can't risk your growing up to think like your dad."

"I told you I've changed. I don't think like that anymore. All I wanted were some shoes that wouldn't hurt your legs."

"Yes, I understand that, but don't you understand that you wanted the shoes and you didn't have enough money so you took them? That's just what your father does. I can't have you in prison, too."

"But I'm not going to do it again!" I was shouting now.

"Jerry, Jerry, listen. Did it ever occur to you to go to a secondhand shop? To a place like Value Village. I would a million times rather have had secondhand sandals than stolen ones."

What could I say to that? I had never thought of a secondhand store. "But what does it matter? What does it matter if I don't want to be a thief and I'm never going to steal again?"

She shook her head. "I can't risk my only son."

"What are you going to do?" I asked her.

54

"I'm going to get a divorce," she said. "I've got an appointment to see a lawyer today."

Everything in me froze. "You said you weren't going to punish me."

"I'm not punishing you. I'm trying to save you. And I'm tired of living like this. It's not good for either one of us."

"You're taking my dad away from me." I got up from the table and walked into my bedroom like a zombie. I lay on my bed and stared at the ceiling for hours and hours. She came to my door to say she was leaving for her appointment.

When she returned, I could hear her putting groceries away in the refrigerator. Later she came to my room again and said dinner was ready.

"I don't want any."

"You haven't eaten all day."

"So?" I turned over in my bed.

"Jerry, I know—"

"Why don't you leave me alone?" I could feel her standing there, but I wouldn't look at her. She left, closing the door quietly behind her.

I slept only a little bit that night. I kept thinking, Where would Dad go when he got out of jail? How were we going to have Christmas? He always got as excited as I did over the presents he gave me. He called me "my boy." What did a dad do in a jail cell when he got his boy taken away from him?

I must have fallen asleep early in the morning, because another knocking woke me up. I lay in bed trying to figure out what was going on. Mom opened my door. "Grace is outside waiting for you."

55

"Tell her I'm not going to school."

"All right," she said. "You can stay home today if you still feel bad. But Monday you're going back to school."

Maybe I would and maybe I wouldn't, I thought to myself. I didn't say anything to her. I just closed my eyes.

Before Mom got up Saturday morning, I climbed into my tree house. I took a sandwich and book with me so I could stay there until she left for work. I still felt awful, but I'd had enough of my bed.

Before long, Grace came up the ladder. "Well, it happened," she said as soon as she'd plopped down beside me. "Just like I knew it would."

"What happened?" I asked.

"The choir director called this morning and kicked me out of choir."

"He told you that?"

"No, he talked to my mom. I don't know what he said. Probably some junk that was supposed to keep Mom from being mad at him while he got rid of me. When she hung up she pretended to be all cheerful. She said I was a good girl for trying hard to sing and I'd been polite to her so I could go to gymnastics on Wednesdays. Big deal, now that the class is half over."

"You've been ripped off." I unwrapped my sandwich. "Want some?"

She leaned over to look at it as I tore it apart. "What's in it?"

"Chicken."

"You always have chicken."

56

"I get whatever's left over in the restaurant's kitchen when Mom's through her shift. Do you want some or not?"

"I guess so." She took it and we chomped on the chicken until Grace said, "What's been the matter with you the last few days anyway? You been sick?"

"No, my mom's divorcing my dad."

"How come? Because he went back to prison?"

"No, because she thinks I'll turn out like him if she lets me stay around him."

"That's dumb." She wiped the mayonnaise off her mouth with the back of her hand. "What gives her that idea?"

"She found out I stole the sandals."

"Whoa! How'd she find out?"

I told Grace the whole story then. She knew about the sandals anyway. When I finished the story, Grace didn't say anything. She just kept picking at a sliver in the floorboard.

I crumpled up my sandwich wrapping and put it in my jacket pocket. "I don't know where he'll go when he gets out."

She pulled at the sliver until it came loose and then tossed it over the side of the tree house. "Seems like a mean thing to do to someone who's locked up."

"It is," I said. "And it's all my fault."

I decided to go to school Monday morning. It couldn't be any worse than staying home. And at school I wouldn't have so much time to think about Dad.

Monday is library day. Mrs. McManus led our class

57

down the hall toward the library. Grace's class was coming the other way, led by Mr. Brewster.

When they were almost ready to pass us, Mr. Brewster came to a halt. "I hear somebody talking," he said in his sergeant's voice. "You just won't be believers, will you? Turn yourselves around and march back to the library and I'd better not hear a sound."

While the kids turned around, Mr. Brewster said to Mrs. McManus, "Sorry to hold you up, but they're going to march until they get it right."

Mrs. McManus nodded to him. "I'll wait here until the library is clear."

We all backed up against the wall. I noticed Summer and Kate were standing by the drinking fountain. Summer had on a yellow baggy sweater, and by the way it hung over her chest I could see she had boobs.

Russell must have checked her out too. When Summer leaned down for a drink of water, Russell slid up behind her, took ahold of the back of her sweater and bra, pulled them out, and then let them go with a snap. As Summer whirled around, Kate said to Russell, "What do you think you're doing, creep?"

"Her name's Summer Day," he said. "I figured she was hot stuff."

Summer's green eyes rounded in her flushed face as she shrank away from him. Russell closed in on her. "Well, Summer, aren't you supposed to be hot?"

It took me five steps to get beside Russell. "Leave her alone."

"Who's gonna make me?"

"I am," I said, and smashed him in the face with my fist. That felt so good, I smashed him again. His head

58

wobbled on his neck. It was like hitting a ripe watermelon, and I smashed him again. Russell went down and I was on him.

"Jerry Johnson!" Mrs. McManus dragged me up by my hair. For an old lady she's got a good arm. "Jerry Johnson, what is going on?"

"Russell started it," Kate said. "He was harassing Summer."

I stood there panting, my muscles straining for action, but Mrs. McManus kept a tight grip on my head. "All of you, into the office. Now."

She steered me by my hair with Russell following us groggily and Kate and Summer trailing him. Mrs. Nettle met us at her office door.

8

Bloody Nose

Mrs. Nettle took one look at Russell and sent him to the nurse's office to take care of his bloody nose. After he left, she brought four chairs up to the front of her desk. She had Kate and Summer sit in the ones near the window and motioned for me to sit at the other end. "Now," she said when she had settled at her desk, "tell me what's been going on."

"Well," Kate began, "Russell came up and popped Summer's bra and when I told him to cut it out, he said Summer must be hot stuff because her name was Summer Day and he kept saying she was hot because she was Summer and this got Summer all upset and Jerry here told him to leave her alone and Russell said, 'Who's gonna make me?' and so Jerry hit him."

Mrs. Nettle drummed her fingers on her desk. Russell came in the door holding a paper towel to his nose. He limped over to the chair beside me and sat down. I don't know why he did the limping act. I hadn't hurt his leg. He probably did it to get Mrs. Nettle's sympathy.

She scooted back a bit, as if she were going to stand

up. "Russell," she said, "will it be all right if I come over and unzip your pants?"

"No!" His eyes were rounder than Summer's had been. "You can't touch me like that."

"Why can't I?"

"Because that's my private—" Russell turned beet red. "You can't touch my pants."

"I can't? I don't understand. You evidently think it's all right to play with Summer's brassiere."

"I wasn't playing with it."

"Oh? What were you doing?"

"I . . ." Russell took a swallow. "I just snapped it."

"Is that all? And you think you can touch a girl's underclothes, but nobody can touch yours?" Mrs. Nettle watched Russell squirm for a couple of seconds before she asked him in a crisp voice, "What is your phone number?"

"My mom's at work."

"Then I will give you a note to take home that says you are not to return to school until you come with one of your parents for a meeting with me." She ripped a paper off a pad on her desk, wrote something on it, and handed the paper to Russell. "Please sit in the outer office until it's time for you to go home."

Kate and Summer had pleased smirks on their faces as they watched Russell slink out of the room. After he left, Mrs. Nettle turned her ammo on me. "Didn't you and I talk last year about ways to solve problems other than using your fists?"

"Yes," I said.

"Hmm. Words don't seem to make a lasting impression on you. Your mother works, right?"

I nodded. I didn't think it would be smart to tell her my mom probably hadn't left for the restaurant yet.

Mrs. Nettle tore another sheet of paper from her pad and wrote something on it before handing it to me. "We'll give you a little time to do some thinking and when you're finished, you can come to school with your mother."

"How long shall I stay home?"

She raised her eyebrows. "How long does it take you to decide not to fight at school? You can start your thinking in the outer office. You remain there until the last bell rings. And I wouldn't advise you to talk to Russell."

"No, ma'am," I agreed. I got up, went into the outer office, and sat two seats away from Russell. He didn't say anything to me. Just kept his head tilted back and the paper towel plastered against his face. I noticed there were splotches of bright red on the towel.

Kate and Summer came out of the principal's office a few minutes later. They were grinning. Each of them gave me a friendly tap on my shoulder as they passed me on their way back to class.

About two hours later, I wished I were back in class. The office chairs are wooden. You sit in them too long and your butt gets tired.

On the bus home all the kids were talking about the fight. Even the little kid with the big glasses stopped staring out the window long enough to look me over. "You really clobbered him, huh?"

"Ya," I said.

After we got off the bus, Grace wanted to know what my mother was going to say.

"Who cares," I said.

"Well, she is your mother."

"So?"

We went by the house that has a bunch of pre-schoolers in it. A tricycle was out on the sidewalk. I put my foot on the seat and gave it a good shove. The tricycle scooted along the sidewalk, over the parking strip, and onto the street, where it dumped over on its side.

"Go get that," Grace demanded.

"You get it if you want it."

"Jerry, the lady in that house belongs to our church. The only money she gets is from her day-care. What if a car runs over the trike?"

"What if it does?"

Grace had her hands on her hips now and was glaring at me. "You're getting just plain mean. You should have socked Russell for hassling Summer, but you didn't have to beat his face to a pulp."

"How many fights you been in, PK?"

Instead of answering me, she marched out into the street, picked up the tricycle, and brought it back in the yard. I went on home without her.

Before I went to bed that night, I put Mrs. Nettle's note on the kitchen table. I'd read it. All it said was that I'd been in a fight and Mom had to come to school to discuss the probable causes of my behavior.

The next morning Mom got up and made breakfast, which she never does unless it's Sunday. While we ate, she told me I didn't have to beat kids up just because I felt bad. I said nothing.

At school I had to sit in a wooden chair again after Mom went in the principal's office. I don't know what they talked about, but when they came out Mrs. Nettle had her arm around Mom's shoulders. I was sent back to class.

Pete took the basketball out at recess and we played one-on-one until Marvin, a loudmouthed kid, joined us. Marvin always tries for impossible shots, which makes him a pain to have on your team. Whenever it was his turn to shoot, I whammed the ball into his stomach.

"Hey, take it easy, Johnson," he complained.

The playground teacher was strolling by about that time. She stopped to give me a frown. As soon as she moved over to the climbing bars, I let Marvin have it in his guts again.

I didn't expect Grace to walk home with me after school. She did, though. She trotted along beside me with her head hidden in the hood of her blue slicker. "Why don't we play chess at my house?" she suggested. "It's too wet to go bike riding."

"Your mom's not home on Tuesdays."

"It's all right. My dad said it was all right."

That's when I should have gotten suspicious. But I was still so bummed out, I wasn't very smart. "I'll play you a game if you're sure it's okay," I agreed. It didn't really matter how I spent the afternoon. There could be a letter from Dad in the mail, but I was afraid of what it might say.

After we'd crossed the street to our block, Grace

slowed down. "Come on in the church with me. I have to get the key to the front door from my dad."

The church is on the corner next to Grace's house. She led me around back and into a hall with doors on each side. I'd never been in this part of the church before. She knocked on one of the doors and after a few seconds Reverend Elliott opened it. He's a big tall man with a black mustache. The ends of the mustache hang to the bottom of his chin. He looked way down at us. "Well, hello there."

"Here's Jerry," Grace said, giving me a shove forward. "See you guys later."

"Hey, wait a minute," I called after her. "You forgot the key."

She stopped halfway down the hall to give me a wave good-bye. "I just remembered. I can get in the back door."

Before I could go after her, Reverend Elliott laid a big paw on my shoulder. "Come on in my study, Jerry. Let's talk a bit."

What about? I wondered as he steered me into the room. A wide desk with a swing-back chair was at one end. Over by the windows were two brown leather chairs. He sat down in one of them and I sat down in the other.

There was a bowl of candy on the table between us. "Have a piece," Reverend Elliott said.

I picked out a dark chocolate. When I crunched it with my teeth, sweet syrup oozed around my tongue. A chocolate-covered cherry. Mom's favorite. Dad always gave her a box of them on Christmas.

66

Reverend Elliott crossed his legs. "I hear you're having some problems."

I swallowed a chunk of cherry before blurting, "Grace blabs too much."

"No, she doesn't. Just to me. And only when she's worried about you. Now tell me, what is she worrying about?"

"I smashed a kid. And trashed a trike. She thinks I'm getting mean."

He pulled on the silky hairs of his mustache with his fingers and thumb. "Hmm. So things haven't been going well with you. Now why is that?"

"My mom's divorcing my dad because she doesn't want me to grow up like him."

"That the only reason she's divorcing him?"

"That's what she told me."

Reverend Elliott tugged on his mustache some more. "I can't quite believe that's the only reason. This is the second time he's gone to prison, right?"

I nodded.

"Do you suppose she's given up on him?"

"I think she has."

"How long was your dad in prison the first time?" he asked.

"Two years," I said.

Reverend Elliott tilted his head back against his leather chair. "Two years, eh? That's a long time to wait and hope. Especially if in the end you decide it was all for nothing when the man you waited for goes right back to prison."

Was this talk supposed to be making me feel better? It was making me feel worse.

67

"Want some more candy?" he asked.

"No," I said. "It might make me sick."

"I wouldn't be surprised. I'd be sick if I believed I was the only reason my parents were getting a divorce."

"Well, maybe I'm not the only reason."

"I doubt that you are. But you're probably going to feel pretty bad when your dad and mother separate and your dad has to go off somewhere alone when he gets out of prison." He smiled down at me. It wasn't a laughing smile. It was a sad smile that made me feel he knew how miserable I was inside.

I squirmed in my chair and he waited a second before he went on. "I want to tell you two true things. If you'll remember them, it'll make your life a little simpler.

"The first thing is that you can change yourself but the chances of your making anyone else change are pretty iffy. And the second thing is that whatever you decide to do, you are responsible for the decision. And . . ." Right here he put in another pause that got my complete attention. "And whatever anyone else decides to do is their responsibility. It isn't yours. Got it?"

"I guess so." If this was a sermon, it sure was weird.

"Now, do you believe those two things?"

"They sound okay."

"All right, then, who's the best person to change your father?"

"He is," I said.

"Who's responsible for your mother's decisions?"

"My mom."

68

Reverend Elliott nodded his head. "And if your mother decides to divorce your father, who's responsible for that decision?"

"She is, but—"

"No 'buts,' " he said.

I stared at my feet.

"Who's responsible for your mother's decisions no matter what they are?"

I looked up into Reverend Elliott's kind brown eyes. "She is," I said.

9

Trust Me

On the way to school the next Wednesday, Grace asked me how many kids rode in Pete's car after gymnastics. "Five, counting Pete," I told her.

"Do you think Mrs. McCartney will take me too?"

"Probably. Why can't your mom drive?"

"She's got a dentist appointment."

We passed the house with the preschoolers in it. A trike was blocking the sidewalk again. I scooted it into the yard.

"You're a good boy," Grace said.

"And you're a bigmouth," I said.

"Only around my dad. And he made you feel better, didn't he?"

I had to admit this was probably true.

Later, while Mrs. McManus was leading us into PE, I asked Pete if Grace could ride with us. He shrugged. "I guess so, but she isn't going to sit on my lap."

She wasn't going to sit on mine either. At least not in front of the other guys. "She can probably squeeze in the backseat," I told Pete.

He wasn't listening. We'd arrived at the gym and he

was staring around the room. "What's Tada got cooked up for us now?"

That was a good question. A third of the gym was taken up with a spooky arrangement of equipment. Near the end wall stood a tall vaulting box with slits in the side for toeholds. In front of that was a long, thick mat. On the other side of the mat was a straddle horse with a padded bar.

Those things didn't bother me. What bothered me was the knotted rope that hung from the ceiling and dangled above the mat. We weren't going to swing from that, were we? I'd had all the swinging I wanted to do. Shudders jerk through me when the broken tree limb even passes across my mind.

"Okay, sit down on the squares, please," Mr. Tada said to us as Mrs. McManus left the gym. We sat down and he led us through the warm-up exercises. All during the head rolls and shoulder shrugs, my eyes kept darting toward the rope. No way was I going to swing from that.

"Now the push-ups," Mr. Tada said. "Try not to touch the floor with your body."

Russell heaved and sweated in the yellow square beside me. What a wienie, I thought to myself. All he could do was take on girls.

"You're doing great," Mr. Tada said. "Sixteen of you kept your bodies off the floor. Now line up in front of the vaulting box."

The pride I'd felt at being one of the sixteen melted as I lined up behind Pete. Fearfully I watched Mr. Tada step on the mat, grab the end of the rope, and keep it in his hand as he climbed up the side of the vaulting

72

box. He positioned himself on top of the box, took hold of a knot on the rope, swung across the mat, and landed neatly on the straddle horse.

"Now," he said, letting the rope go. "Each of you guys take a try at that."

I shrank smaller and smaller as the kids in front of Pete peeled off for their turns. Most of them managed to swing across the mat to the straddle horse. Kate didn't give a big enough push off the vaulting box and dribbled above the center of the mat. Russell shot off the box, landed straight up on the horse, and beat his chest like Tarzan.

When there were only two kids left in front of Pete, I kneeled down to retie my shoes. Eric had finished his swing and was running past me to the end of the line. I trotted after him like I'd just finished my turn too.

Up ahead I could see Pete craning his neck to find out what was happening with me. I crouched down and retied my shoes again, trying to make it look like I was having a real problem with the laces. Mr. Tada tapped me on the shoulder. "You aren't taking a turn?" he asked quietly.

"No." I stood up and flexed my wrist in front of him. "I'm not sure if my wrist is strong enough yet."

"How did you get hurt?"

"I held on to a branch to swing out of my tree house and the branch broke."

"Oh, I see. That would make you nervous about the rope all right."

Before I could get really embarrassed about his putting it so plain, he took me by my arm. "Trust me," he

73

whispered, and led me down the line of kids and onto the mat.

"Now you guys are going to work in pairs," he announced, still holding my arm. "You can pretend you're Indiana Jones and rescue your partner. Starting at the head of the line, count off in twos."

The kids counted off in twos. Summer, who was at the end of the line, was left with no partner. "Jerry will be your partner when I'm done with him," he assured her.

"Get on top of the vaulting box, Jerry." He let go of my arm and, with all the kids watching, there was nothing else for me to do but climb on the box. I stood there sweating while Mr. Tada took the rope up the straddle horse.

"Now you guys watch, because it's all a matter of timing. You ready, Jerry?"

I nodded. Mr. Tada pushed off the horse, swung over the mat, and, as he came up to the box, turned the rope toward me. I grabbed onto a knot and we swung back to the horse together, landing on the padded bar.

"How did you like it?" he asked me, his black eyes shining.

"It was a blast," I told him.

I waited beside the mat to watch Pete try to rescue Kate. It took two tries because the first time Kate was late grabbing the rope and Pete swung back without her. After I walked to my place behind Summer in the line, she turned to give me a quick frightened glance. "I'll never be able to do it."

"Sure you will," I said. "Just trust me."

Eric and Robert were the next partners. On their

74

first swing they made it together to the straddle horse and raised their arms in victory while we clapped. Russell and Wayne had to drop on the mat because they lost their momentum struggling for a toehold on the horse.

When our turn came, Summer wouldn't move. I shoved her over to the vaulting box, whispering to her rigid back, "Trust me. Trust me."

I guess she did, because when I swung up beside her, she grabbed the knot I pushed toward her and hung on until we reached the horse. The kids clapped. I bowed, jumped down, and held my hand out to Summer. "How'd you like it?" I asked.

"Scary," she said.

In the after-school class, Grace didn't think the rope swing was scary. She rescued Mari, Mari rescued her, she rescued Mari, until Mr. Tada suggested they go over to the cheese mat and practice headsprings so the rest of us could get a turn on the rope.

When Pete's mom picked us up, she agreed to give Grace a ride home with us, lucky for me. Mrs. McCartney had barely pulled out of the school parking lot when she started on her questions. "Does your dad commute to Monroe every day, Jerry?"

"Watch the road, Mom," Pete said.

Grace leaned forward from her perch between Kate and Mari. "My dad only has to walk across our backyard to get home, but he hardly ever stays after dinner. He's too busy counseling people from our church."

This interested Mrs. McCartney. "That many people need help?" she asked.

"Yes," Grace said. "Some are out of work. Some have trouble with their kids or their husbands."

"Is it mostly women he counsels?" Mrs. McCartney was really getting into it.

"Oh, no," Grace said coolly. "Some nights it's all teenagers."

"Teenagers? What do they have to come for? Pregnancy?"

"Mom," Pete said. "You just went through a stop sign. Turn left at the next corner."

Fortunately, Mrs. McCartney paid attention to her driving until she let Grace and me off in front of the Elliotts' house. As we watched the car go down the road, I said to Grace, "What a nosy witch."

"Right," Grace agreed. "You have to be real careful what you talk about around her. She spends half her life on the phone. When she calls our house, my mom tries to pretend she's late for an appointment. Mom says she gets a headache trying to make sure she doesn't say any little thing that Mrs. McCartney can turn into gossip."

I don't have to worry about phone calls, I thought to myself after I said good-bye to Grace and walked across my yard. Now that Dad was gone, the phone hardly rang and the silent house seemed empty and hollow without him.

The next day was Thursday, one of my mother's days off. She made chicken-fried steak for dinner, which she knows I like. I didn't tell her it was good. I was still burning about her telling me she was divorcing Dad because she believed he'd turn me into a thief.

On Sunday she got all dressed up like she used to when she visited Dad at the reformatory. I looked up from the funnies when she came into the living room. "How come you're so fancy?" I asked.

"I'm going to Monroe to let your dad know my plans." She didn't look down at me on the floor. Just busied herself checking in her purse and taking out her car keys.

"Dad already knows about the sandals," I said.

Her eyes widened. "You told him?"

"Yes, and when I told him, he said he'd rather kill himself than have me in prison. So don't bother blaming me for your decision. Your decisions are your responsibility."

She snapped her purse shut. "I know that."

You haven't been acting like it, I wanted to snap back, but she was already opening the front door. She closed it behind her without saying good-bye.

10

Letters from Prison

The first letter I got from Dad came the day before my birthday. He didn't mention the divorce, but he sent me fifteen dollars and said he wanted me to buy something for my bike. "I've been thinking you could use a headlight. Or a lambskin cover for your seat. That'd keep your hind end warm, heh-heh."

Dad always puts "Heh-hehs" in his letters. "But maybe," he wrote on, "fifteen bucks won't get you a seat cover. I wish I could send you more, but I have to wait until there's an opening for a better-paying job. I'll try and save plenty for Christmas so we can celebrate. You won't have to worry about me coming back to this hole. They threw the book at old Rattler."

His letter ended with "I miss you my boy. Love, Yr Dad."

I was sitting at the kitchen table, drinking a Pepsi and thinking about Christmas, when Grace banged on the back door. After I let her in, she said in one breath, "Matt's driving to the mall and I'm going because Mom wants me to buy her some yarn and Matt said you could come too."

79

Monkey See. Monkey Do.

I thought fast. If I went to Sears for my present, I wouldn't have to ask Mom to take me anywhere. I grabbed my coat and left with Grace.

Grace had to get the yarn at Frederick and Nelson's. I stood around while she pawed through the rolls of colors, trying to match the sample she'd brought. When she had her package, we rushed over to Sears. Matt was picking up some cassette tapes, and he'd said to meet him back at his car in a half hour.

It took me about twenty minutes to decide what I wanted for my bike. Grace was in favor of a squeeze-bottle rack. I couldn't make up my mind between an automatic turn signal and a headlight. I finally decided on the headlight.

We ran across the parking lot through the wind and rain to Matt's car. He wasn't even there. We stood around on the wet pavement until he sauntered up like it was no big deal that water was pouring off our hair and down our necks.

When we got in the car, though, he pulled a towel out from under the front seat and tossed it back to Grace. "You should have worn your slicker. You know you can't trust Northwest weather."

"You mean," she told him, rubbing her long black hair with the towel, "I can't trust you to be on time."

Matt didn't say anything more. Neither did we because he'd shoved one of his new cassettes in the tape deck and hard rock blasted out of the four speakers that hung from the corners of the roof. Grace finished drying her hair and passed the towel to me.

We had both stopped shivering by the time Matt swerved into their driveway. He got out first and held the door open for us. The back of his car is really cramped. In the front you sit with your legs out straight. In the back you rest your chin on your knees. To get out you have to crawl over the front seat like a spider.

"Thanks for the ride," I said, stretching up into the rain to relieve my muscles.

"No problem," he said.

I jumped the bushes between our houses and took the headlight into the garage, put the batteries in it, and attached it to my bike. It looked so great, I had to ride the bike around the inside of the garage to try out the beam.

Before I went to bed, I left the box on the kitchen table and dumped the sack and receipt in the garbage. That way Mom could see the pictures of the headlight on the box and wonder how I got it. Served her right for not believing I'd changed.

The next day was Sunday and she was up when I got up. "Happy birthday," she said.

I gave her a quick nod and pulled a box of Rice Krispies out of the cupboard. She smiled at me from the kitchen table. "I made you some waffles."

I didn't want to eat her waffles. I didn't even want to talk to her. "Cereal's okay," I mumbled, putting the box on the table and going to the refrigerator for some milk.

"No." She got up and opened the oven door wide. "See? They're all ready."

"You eat them," I told her.

"Jerry! It's your birthday. I made them for you." She took the plate of waffles out of the oven and

81

placed it on the table between a knife and fork. There was a glass of orange juice, syrup, and butter there too. I didn't want any of it, but I wasn't certain how rude I could be. I'd hardly spoken to her since she said she was going to divorce Dad.

"I'm not really hungry. I think I'll take a bike ride." I shoved the quart of milk back in the refrigerator, but before I could open the kitchen door, she pulled on my hand.

"Jerry, it's your birthday. I've got a present for you. Don't you want my present?"

How could I say no? I sat down at the table while she went to get it.

"Here," she said, giving me a long white package tied with blue ribbon. "I hope you like it."

It was a skateboard. Who was I supposed to ride a skateboard with? Grace didn't have a skateboard.

Mom's face puckered with disappointment. "Don't you like it?"

"Sure. It's neat." I turned it over and spun the wheels.

She sat down beside me. "I saw some boys outside the restaurant riding these. They were going really fast and one of the boys flipped his skateboard around and went the other way without even stopping. I thought of how coordinated you are and that you could do that too."

"Okay, I'll go out and try it."

"Eat first before these get cold." She pushed the waffles closer to me. "You got a present from your dad, huh?"

"He sent me some money."

82

"How did you get to the store?"

"The Elliotts took me." I still hadn't picked up my knife or my fork. I could feel she wanted to hand them to me. Instead she shoved the butter plate next to the waffles.

"Where did you and the Elliotts go? I saw the box when I got home and figured you'd heard from your dad."

I stared straight into her eyes. "I thought you'd figure I stole the headlight."

"Oh, Jerry, I didn't think that. I know the divorce will be hard on you, but your dad won't change. I used to hope he would, but he's not going to."

I was sitting back in my chair now, looking her up and down. "And you don't believe I can change either."

"Yes, I do. That's not it at all. I just don't want him to influence you." She sank her teeth into her upper lip and blinked fast. She could go ahead and cry for all I cared.

"So if he's around me, I might start stealing again."

"Oh, no. Oh."

I had to force myself to stay cold while I watched the tears that were wobbling in her eyes spill over and slide down her cheeks.

"Jerry, your dad isn't the only one who loves you. I love you too."

"And what's he supposed to do on Christmas? Go to the Salvation Army?"

"No, a divorce doesn't mean we can't see him. We'll invite him here for Christmas morning."

That's big of you, I wanted to tell her, but her wet,

white face made her look like she'd just been punished and I couldn't say it. Instead, I picked up my knife and spread butter on the cold waffles.

Dad wrote me every week and I wrote him back. When gymnastics ended and Mr. Tada started us on basketball, I told Dad how Pete and I always tried to get on the same side and cream the other kids. Grace's class challenged us to a game, and Mrs. McManus let us skip math so we could have gym in the morning with them.

Our class voted for the members of our first team. Of course, Pete and I were on it. Mr. Brewster got mad when we were ten points ahead of his team and started yelling, "Come on, you lunkheads, get in there and score." Grace told her mother about Brewster calling his kids "lunkheads."

She was still trying to get out of his room. So was Clayton. He'd had his ear pierced and was wearing an earring, which was driving Brewster wild, but Mrs. Nettle wouldn't send Clayton home. She said an earring didn't obstruct the learning process.

Clayton told me all this while we were standing on the sidelines watching the second teams play. Clayton was the highest scorer in his room, but I guess in Brewster's mind that didn't make up for the earring. I asked Clayton what his parents thought about his purple hair and earring. He said they didn't care. They figured it was his body.

After I wrote about Clayton to Dad, he wrote back that some of the guys at the reformatory had earrings. He said that earrings weren't as popular as tattoos,

84

though. Dad had a tattoo of a snake on his arm. I inked a snake on my arm to see how it would look. I decided I'd rather have an earring.

As Christmas came nearer Dad got more and more excited about leaving prison. "Only ten more days to go," he wrote. "I've missed too much time with you and I'm not taking a chance of missing any more. I've been getting some counseling and doing some thinking and I think I'll try for a job as a salesman when I get out. I'm a friendly guy and I know how to butter up people so I might as well use these abilities in a straight job. Right?"

Right, I thought. But I doubted that he'd be able to butter up Mom. I stayed awake nights worrying about how he'd feel going off alone after spending Christmas morning with me.

11

Home for Christmas

Grace and I found Dad sitting on the front steps three days before Christmas. I dropped my bike and rushed up to the porch. He grabbed me by the shoulders, took a long look into my face, and smothered me in a bear hug. "My boy, you've grown. Just three months and you've grown again."

"A half inch," I told him. "I measure myself in the nurse's office."

"You come up to my nose. You're going to be bigger than I am." He let go of my shoulders and beamed down at me.

I took a step back, stumbling on the large white carton he'd left on the steps. "What's in the box?"

"That's a pizza." He nodded at Grace, who was standing by her bike watching us. "You want to have dinner with us, blue eyes?"

"No thanks, I have to go home. See ya, Jerry." Grace wheeled her bike down the sidewalk and over to her house.

"She's a pretty little thing," Dad said.

He followed me around the side of our house while I

put my bike away. When I took my key out to unlock the back door, he took his out too. "I guess I better leave this for Lily since I don't live here anymore." He tossed the key on the kitchen table.

I kept my attention on taking off my jacket and dumping it on a chair. The last thing I wanted to do was talk about the divorce. It turned out that I didn't have to because what Dad wanted to talk about was his new job.

He told me all the details as we porked down the pizza. "Jim's Appliance Store is the biggest one in Everett. He hired me to help out with the holiday rush and this morning he told me he was keeping me on for the sale after Christmas. Jim's got a deal where any salesman who sells ten refrigerators in a month gets a bonus. Give me the customers and I can sell ten refrigerators easy." Dad paused to wipe the tomato sauce off his mouth with a paper napkin.

"Why didn't you come over or call me as soon as you got out? I hung around the house until today when Grace asked me to go bike riding."

"I wanted to have a job and an apartment before I came over here." He smiled at me thoughtfully. "A couple times I almost picked up the phone to call you. But it's better this way. Now I've got a place for you to visit. It isn't fancy. Just a big room and a bath above a garage, but it's only a mile away."

"That's neat." I wasn't sure how often Mom was going to let me visit him, but I didn't bring this up. I concentrated on getting another slice of pizza from the box by pulling the stringy cheese apart with my fingers.

88

"You'll have to bike up to my place until I can buy a car." He smiled again, showing the gap between his front teeth that was the same as mine. "Have to put my money on Christmas first."

"I made all my presents," I told him.

I stuck my presents under the tree before I went to bed Christmas Eve. It seemed as if I'd hardly gotten asleep before Dad was pounding on the front door. "How come you're not up yet?" he asked when I let him in. "It's seven o'clock."

"But it's still dark," I mumbled as I headed out of the room to put on my clothes.

Dad had the tree lighted and was sitting on the edge of the big chair waiting for us when I came back in the living room followed by Mom. She was wearing her long pink robe. Her hair was combed, but she didn't have any makeup on. I think she looks better without any. That's probably what Dad thought too.

His eyes were shining as he said softly, "Merry Christmas, Lily."

"Merry Christmas, Jerry," she said back to him.

I sat down by the tree. "Who's going to be Santa Claus?"

"You be Santa Claus." Mom settled on the davenport and carefully folded her robe over her legs to hide her nightgown.

"Okay! Let's see. Here's one for Jerry Senior from Jerry Junior." I handed the package to Dad and watched as he tore off the wrapping.

"This is great!" he said. "A mask of your face. Great!" He turned the white plaster of paris mask

89

around in his hands, examining it carefully. "But how come it's got lashes sticking out the back of the eyes?"

"Those aren't supposed to be there," I explained. "Pete was supposed to smear Vaseline all over my face. He didn't put enough on my eyelashes, though, so when he pulled the mask off, half my eyelashes came off with it. See?" I pointed to my eyelid, which looked like mice had been nibbling around the rim.

Mom shivered. "Didn't that hurt?"

"Ya, when he pulled them out."

"I'll hang this on my wall," Dad said.

"Let me see it." Mom reached out her hands. Dad crossed the room, sat down beside her, and handed her the mask.

This was like old times. My insides swelled with happy Christmas spirit. "And here's a present for you, Mom, from your favorite son."

She gave Dad his mask and carefully unwrapped her present. "Oh! A silhouette of your head. How lovely, and you matted it in blue. It will match my bedroom."

"I know. I tried to pick out paper that was the same color as your quilt." I didn't add that this was Summer's idea.

Dad had moved close to Mom to see the picture too. "How'd you make this?" he asked me.

"Well, you stand next to a wall that has a sheet of paper on it. Then another kid turns on a lamp so the shadow of your profile shows on the paper. Then the kid draws around the shadow while you're standing there. Summer was doing it for me. She's kind of a dingy girl, but she's good in art."

90

"I guess she is." Mom pointed under the tree. "Why don't you open that big green box now."

The tag said, "To Jerry Jr. from Mom." I couldn't figure out what could be inside. "A leather jacket! Whoa!" I sprang to my feet, pulling the black jacket out of the tissue paper. "Aw right! How do I look?"

Mom and Dad admired me as I shrugged my shoulders into the jacket and turned this way and that. "Wow! Neat." I went in the bathroom to see myself in the long mirror that hung on the door. Too cool!

I strutted back to the living room and gave Mom a kiss. She laughed. "I guess that gift was a success."

"You better believe it," I told her. "And now, another one for you. This one's from Dad."

It was two packages tied together with red ribbon. A bottle of perfume and a box of chocolate-covered cherries. "How nice." Mom smiled at Dad. "You remembered what I like."

He was leaning toward her like he hoped he'd get a kiss. She didn't give him one. I hurried on to the next present. "This is for you, Dad. From Mom."

It was a fruitcake.

"We made them at the restaurant this year," Mom told him. "Now that you're baching, I thought you could use a little dessert."

"Sure can. Thanks." He dumped the fruitcake beside him on the davenport.

The next presents were small ones for me from Mom. Socks and junk.

"Now," Dad said, his face lighting up, "open the last one, Jerry."

It was another big flat box. Only red this time. Before I got the wrappings off, I couldn't guess what this one was either. "Okay! A video set. Just what I need." I checked out the control pads, power pack, cartridges, adapter, and control deck until I came to some wires wrapped in plastic, which I held up to Dad. "What are these for?"

He hopped off the davenport. "They're pigtail wires. I'll show you how to set the whole thing up."

We pulled the TV away from the wall together, and Dad hitched up the equipment. When he had everything turned on, we pushed the TV back and Dad held out both control pads. "See, you push the top of the cross down when you want to shoot up. When you want to shoot low, you push here and when you want to shoot to the right, you push here and when you want to shoot to the left, you—"

"I know. I know. It's just like Pete's." I grabbed a pad from Dad. "Come on. Let's play."

He shoved the cartridge of an airplane game into the control deck. When the game came on the screen, Dad and I were supposed to get our fighter planes off the ground. He got his plane up right away. I had barely gotten mine in the air when he came down on top of it and blasted it to pieces.

"Gotcha!" he yelled.

"This time," I said, pointing my finger at him. "Just wait until I catch on."

I lost three more times before I had the hang of it. In the fourth game I chased his airplane all over the screen until I got mine maneuvered below his and shot it in the belly. "You're dead!" I screamed as his plane went down in flames.

92

"Lucky shot!" he hollered. "You won't get to do that again."

Mom bent down between us and handed Dad a cup of coffee and me a cup of cocoa. "I'm going to drop some presents off at the restaurant. I imagine you two will be all right for an hour."

"Sure. Thanks," Dad said.

"He's going to be one beaten man when you get back," I told her.

She ruffled my hair and went out the door with her presents.

Dad and I were taking a food break when she came back. As soon as we heard her car, he smoothed his hair and I brushed the toast crumbs off the davenport. She came in all smiles, carrying some more packages.

"What'd you get?" I asked.

"Oh, just some little things from my friends."

The packages didn't look so little to me. She dropped them in the big chair before she asked Dad if he'd like a ride home.

He jumped to his feet. "Fine. Fine."

"Can I come too?" I wanted to know.

"Of course," she said.

Dad turned around to me when Mom pulled the car up in front of his garage apartment. "See, you go up those stairs on the side. There's a balcony that faces the house. That's where my front door is." He nodded to Mom. "Okay if I have Jerry over next Saturday night?"

"Certainly. As long as you keep your job he can visit you." She sounded like a schoolteacher.

Dad got out of the car and waved a hand to me. I

climbed into the front seat. "What's this about I can visit Dad if he has a job?"

She eased the car away from the curb. "That's the deal. I've agreed to let him see you as long as he is legitimately employed."

"Sounds like blackmail," I said. "And you don't think I'll get contaminated?"

"No." She was keeping her eyes on the road.

I let it drop there. I wasn't really mad at her anymore. The leather jacket felt great hanging on my shoulders and it was Christmas after all.

Hotshot

When I got over to Dad's Saturday night, he was all hopped up about his job. He'd sold two refrigerators and a washing machine that day. "Wanna go around to the wrecking yards tomorrow to look for an old junker I can fix up?"

"Sure," I said, "but how will you get it back here?"

He pulled out his wallet. "Easy. A couple of these bills for the junker and a couple more for the tow."

I craned my neck over his fat wallet. "Gee, you've got a lot in there."

"Payday. Here. Have a fin." He pulled out a five-dollar bill and handed it to me.

"Thanks," I said, stuffing it in my jeans. No more dried-up chicken sandwiches next week. I'd be able to buy my lunch.

We walked to the movie in Snohomish that night. The next morning we rode the bus to the wrecking yard. Or wrecking yards. We had to walk back from the bus stop past the section for Japanese cars, past the Volkswagens, and past the Fords until we came to the Chevrolets. Camaros were Dad's favorites.

I was glad I had my leather jacket because it was freezing out. Frost was still covering the windshields on the cars. Or on most cars. The Camaro Dad picked had a smashed windshield. It also had a caved-in door, crushed fender, and no grille.

"What do you want this one for? It's totaled." I was shivering beside Dad while he was peering inside the car.

"Because it's got keys in it so the engine must run." He climbed in the car and started up the motor. After it'd been running a few minutes, he jumped out, lifted up the hood, and checked the engine. A man in overalls came up to us. "Nothing's wrong with the engine," he said. "This car just needs bodywork."

Dad's head was still under the hood. "How much?"

"Four-fifty, including the tow."

"Will you throw in a door, windshield, fender, and grille?"

"I can't do that," the man said. "I can't strip another car. You can have this and the one over there for six hundred."

Dad straightened up and slammed the hood. "No way. I can get one with a new paint job at a used-car lot for that."

"A beater five years older."

Dad grinned at the man.

The man looked down at his feet. Dad kept grinning and I kept shivering. Finally, the man said, "Well, I shouldn't do it, but you can have this Camaro and strip that one over there for four seventy-five. But it will cost you extra for the tow."

"Naw, you can do better."

96

The man shook his head, sighed, and shook his head
again. "Well, I'll throw in the tow if you're ready to
leave before noon. I've got another job at one
o'clock."

"We'll be ready if we can use your tools," Dad told
him.

The man nodded, and we followed him into his
office for the tools. I wished I could stay in there because the man had a heater warming up the place. Dad
handed me a crowbar, though, and I had to walk back
out to the wrecking yard with him.

"What are you going to do with this bar?" I asked
when we got to his Camaro.

"Pry the fender off the tire," he said. "You can start
doing that while I get this door."

The whole passenger side of the car was bashed in.
It must have been hit by a truck. A ten-ton truck. It
took us over an hour to pull off the door and windshield. It took us another hour to strip the car across
the lane.

Dad piled the good door, grille, windshield, and
fender inside his Camaro while the man backed the
tow truck down the lane. I stood blowing on my fingers until the Camaro was hitched up and I could
climb in the truck beside Dad. Lucky for my frozen feet
that the tow truck had a heater.

When we got to Dad's place, the truck driver
dropped the Camaro neatly beside the garage. "We
better get something to eat before we start working,"
Dad said.

I ate my pork and beans as slowly as I could. Too
slow for Dad. "I'll start pounding out dents," he told

me. "When you're finished, come on out and you can start sanding."

That's what we did until it was almost dark. By the time I'd ridden my bike home my fingers were raw. Mom was in the living room watching TV. I held my hands out to her. "The radio says it's going to snow. I need some warm gloves."

"So you do," she said. "I'll pick up a pair before work tomorrow."

It snowed all week. I wore my new gloves to help Grace build a snowwoman in her front yard. Grace poked twigs above the eyes for eyelashes. The thing looked ridiculous.

Dad had to work at Jim's Appliance Store on Saturday and half of Sunday. He had me bus down to meet him Sunday so we could have dinner together. I sat on the bookkeeper's desk and watched Dad total up his sales for the day. "Beat fifteen hundred again, Eva," he told the bookkeeper.

She raised her eyebrows at me. "Your Dad's a hotshot."

Two women and two little kids had come into the store. Another salesman trapped them before they got halfway down the middle aisle. "What can I do you for?" he asked with a sappy smile.

Dad shook his head at me. Not cool.

The younger woman said she was looking for a convection oven. The salesman steered her over to the stoves. The little girl grabbed the older woman's hand and pulled her the other way. "Look at this refrigerator, Grandma. It's pretty. You should get it and throw away your old broken one."

The grandma stroked the shiny metal handles. "Yes, it is pretty."

"Look. It's got an ice maker," the boy said. "I wish ours had an ice maker."

"It would be nice for iced tea all right," his grandma said.

Dad's head had raised up like a bird dog's. He slid smoothly away from the bookkeeper's desk and over to the grandma. "You've picked out the best buy in the store. This refrigerator's on sale this week for seven ninety-five." He left out the part that everything in the store was on sale every week.

The woman backed up a bit. "We were just looking."

Dad opened the refrigerator door and nodded at the little kids. "It's a perfect size for you and your children."

"Oh, they're not my children. They're my grandchildren."

Dad stared at the woman as if he were completely confused. "Your *grand*children?"

"Yes." The woman was smiling self-consciously.

Dad shrugged. "Well, I guess women get younger every year while we men just get bald."

"Oh, you're not bald." The woman was laughing now.

Dad smoothed his hand over his brown hair. "Maybe not yet but every time I look in the mirror it seems like my forehead's grown another inch."

What a con man, I thought to myself. He'll have that grandma reeled in in no time.

He did, too. The kids' mother came back without

99

having bought her stove. "What do you need a new refrigerator for?" she asked the grandma sharply.

"Because I'm sick of having to slam the door of my old one to keep it shut," the grandma said just as sharply.

Not a muscle moved in Dad's face as he continued writing up the order while the women argued. The bookkeeper phoned in for a credit check, which must have been good because she wrote an authorization number on the Visa slip. Dad handed the grandma a copy of the slip and the order form.

"We'll have your new refrigerator out to you the first thing tomorrow morning and haul away your old one. Before the men leave they'll have the ice maker up and running, right, son?" Dad patted the head of the little boy, who smiled happily back at him.

As the family went out the door I heard the little boy say, "Can I stay all night with you, Grandma?"

Dad picked up his tally sheet. "That makes twenty-three hundred for today."

We ate at a Chinese restaurant before catching the bus. I got off the bus at my stop and Dad stayed on to ride to his. I'd invited him to watch TV at my house, but he said he had a feeling that wouldn't please Lily. He said he'd let her get used to him as a working stiff before he came around again. I figured that was a smart move.

He had the next Saturday off and we worked all day on the car. He bored holes in the side so he could pull out the dented metal. After he filled the holes I sanded them down with an electric sander he'd rented.

By the time it got dark, we had the car in one piece. I

100

stood back and looked it over before he drove me home. If you didn't count the green door and all the gray patches, it looked pretty good. "It's going to look a lot better," Dad said, "when we get it painted."

"Paint it black." I wanted it to be as cool as Matt's car.

"If you'll come over next weekend while I'm working and give it one more sanding, I'll paint it black."

"It's a deal," I said.

13

Sleepin' In

I was over at Dad's house by nine-thirty Saturday morning. He'd given me a key so I could get the tools to work on the car. I was just inside his door and stooping to pick up the sander when someone turned over in the bed.

I'd thought the darkened room was empty and the bed covers were rumpled. I tiptoed across the carpet to look down at the pillows. Dad was lying there sound asleep.

I put my hand on his shoulder. "Dad, are you sick?"

He half opened his eyes and squinted at me. "Oh. Hi, Jerry. What time is it?"

"It's almost ten. I thought you had to work today."

"I do." He raised up on his elbow, shook a cigarette out of the pack on the table, lit it, and took a drag before he dropped back on his pillows. "Listen, do me a favor and call up Jim's Appliance and tell them I've got the flu. The Everett phone book's right there on the table."

"Do you really have the flu?"

"Naw, I got playing pool down at the tavern last

103

night and didn't get home until three." He gave me his pumpkin-tooth grin. "Made a little money, though, beating the pants off those dudes. Cleared the table four times."

I didn't tell him that was neat. I also didn't ask him why he couldn't get up and go to work late. I knew he thought weekends were party time, so I just called the store and told the bookkeeper Dad was sick.

She said, "Oh, my goodness, that's too bad. I hope he feels better soon. Tom's going in for a hernia operation on Thursday."

I said I thought Dad only had the twenty-four-hour flu. The bookkeeper said she'd heard that was going around. After I hung up, I asked Dad, "Who's Tom?"

"He's Jim's star salesman. Or he is when he isn't bent over holding his guts in."

"The bookkeeper said he's getting an operation Thursday. She hopes you're going to be back by then."

"No sweat." He took a last drag on his cigarette, leaned over to grind out the butt in the ashtray, and gave me another grin as he tossed his covers back. "How about we ride the junker down to Denny's and get ourselves some pancakes? Then we can come back here and get it ready for a paint job. I need the day off anyway."

Dad went in the bathroom to take a shower. I sat down on a chair to worry. He wouldn't mess up again, would he? He hadn't even been out two months.

As soon as I woke up the next morning, I called Dad. There was no answer, so I figured he'd gone to work.

Before Mom could come out of her bedroom and ask me any questions about him, I went up to my tree house. I took my sleeping bag with me because it was freezing out.

It wasn't long before I spotted Grace going toward my front door. I yelled down at her, "I'm up here!"

She peered through the branches. "What are you doing there? It's six degrees. Come on over to my house and play me some chess."

"What about church?"

"Mom and I just got back."

Mrs. Elliott made me nervous. Grace and the Reverend had never told her about my Dad's record, but I was always afraid she'd find out. Whenever I was around her, I felt like I should be hanging my head.

"Come on!" Grace insisted. "My feet are frozen."

I climbed down and joined her.

"You're scared of my mom, aren't you?" she said as we walked over to her yard.

"I'm not scared of her. But what will she do if she finds out my dad's an ex-convict?"

"She'll put up an eight-foot fence between our houses." Grace gave me a jab in the shoulder. "Come on. Lighten up. Who's going to tell her?"

Grace and I had barely gotten the chessboard set up when Mrs. Elliott came in the room with root beer and cookies. She watched Grace push her pawn forward, me push mine forward, Grace shove another pawn out, and me put my chin in my hand to ponder the next move. She watched as Grace held her finger on her rook, trying to decide if that was the right attack.

105

She watched Grace take her finger off her rook and me rub my fingers over my mouth to hide a smile.

Mrs. Elliott shook her head. "This has got to be the most boring game."

"Why don't you buy me a Nintendo then?" Grace asked, sliding her bishop diagonally across the board.

Mrs. Elliott left the room and I rubbed a smile away from my mouth again. Grace was going to lose.

"Just luck," Grace said after I checkmated her.

"You wish," I said. "The fact is my brain's larger than yours."

"It is not." She didn't think this was funny at all.

She thought it was even less funny when I beat her again. Instead of claiming it was luck, she leaned back in her chair, kicked up her feet, and sent the chessboard flying through the air. Mrs. Elliott ran into the living room when she heard the wooden board clatter to the floor. "What is going on?"

"I lost," Grace said.

Mrs. Elliott placed her hands on her hips and glared down at Grace. "Shame on you. That's no way to treat your company. Pick everything up and come in the kitchen and help me."

Grace and I got down on our hands and knees to pick up the pieces and put them inside the board. She folded it shut and snapped the little brass hook in place. "Guess that's all the fun for today."

"I guess," I agreed. "See you tomorrow."

When I got home, Mom was in the living room reading the Sunday paper. I took off my jacket and asked her for the funnies.

"Here you are," she said, handing me the comics section. "How's your dad's car coming along?"

"Fine," I told her. "It's ready to paint."

She raised her eyebrows, but didn't ask me any more questions. I stretched out on the floor and concentrated on the funnies.

After I got home from school on Wednesday, Dad phoned me. "Got the car all taped up to paint. Wanna come over and watch?"

"Didn't you have to work today?"

"Nope, I get Wednesday off this week. But that's the only day, so if you want to see a blue junker turn into a black beauty you better bike over here."

"I'll be there in twenty minutes."

It took me twenty-five. Dad had the car in the garage. The windows, handles, and headlights were covered with tape. Dad was wearing goggles and had already started to spray-paint one side.

"Close the door quick," he said. "I don't want any dirt to blow in here."

I closed the garage door and sat down on a box to watch. Gradually, gradually, the blue junker with the green door and the gray patches turned into a sleek black Camaro. "Whoa! Beautiful," I told Dad as we stepped back to examine his paint job.

A small redheaded man opened the garage door.

"Close it quick," I warned him.

"Hi, there, Mr. Simmons," Dad said. "This is my son, Jerry."

Mr. Simmons shook my hand and then turned to admire the car. "I can't believe this is the same wreck you had towed in here. My wife wanted me to tell you

107

to have it hauled right back out. Any chance you can do this to my car? How much would you charge me?"

"About a month's rent."

Mr. Simmons tapped his thumb on his lips. "Hmm, I'd sure like to have it done. I'll have to talk it over with my wife."

After Mr. Simmons left, Dad and I cleaned out the paint sprayer and went up to his room to eat. "It's going to be so neat riding around in that Camaro," I kept saying between bites of my TV dinner. I could just see Grace's eyes bugging out when we drove up in front of my house. Dad's car was even cooler than Matt's.

Dad didn't answer his phone when I tried to call him Saturday night. Sunday morning I talked Grace into another bike ride and led her around the streets toward Dad's place. I didn't think he'd sleep in again, especially since that would make the appliance store short two salesmen. Still, the worry kept circling around my mind.

The nearer we got to Dad's block, the faster I pedaled. "Slow down," Grace hollered from behind me. "I've only got a five-speed, you know."

I slowed down as soon as I saw the black Camaro parked beside the garage. Maybe he left it there and took the bus. Maybe he sprayed on the second coat and the paint wasn't dry. Maybe he wasn't in his room asleep.

"Why are we stopping?" Grace pulled up in the driveway by dragging a foot on the ground. "Wow. Is that your dad's car?"

108

"Yes," I said, "and I don't know why it's here." I parked my bike and headed for the garage stairs.

Grace was right behind me. "Does he work on Sundays?"

"He's supposed to." The blinds were closed on the windows beside the door. I swore as I turned the key in the lock. "He better not be home."

"What's buzzing?" she asked, following me into the darkened room.

I walked across the carpet and turned the alarm off. Dad was flat on his back on the bed with his mouth wide open.

"Gol, he sure snores loud enough," Grace whispered.

I lifted his arm and gave it a rough shake.

"Unh. Unh," he mumbled, tugging his arm away and turning over to his side.

I punched him in the shoulder. "Wake up! It's past twelve-thirty."

"What?" Dad flopped to his back. "What? Oh, Jerry. What's up?"

"One o'clock is up," I said.

He stared at me blankly a minute, then jerked around to check his electric clock. "The blasted alarm didn't work."

"It worked. I just turned it off."

"Oh." He peered across the room. "Hello there, blue eyes. I must have slept in."

Grace shifted her feet around. She didn't seem to know whether to leave or stay.

"Better call the store, Jerry," Dad said. "Tell them I'm fixing a flat tire and I'll be there in a half hour."

109

"They're going to believe it takes all morning to fix a flat?"

"Well, it could if I were out on the road. Tell them you're with me and you're calling from a gas station."

I didn't want to do it. I wanted to tell him to call himself. But then I thought that he probably didn't have any pajamas on and Grace was still inside the door.

I called the appliance store. Jim answered. I gave him the long spiel about the tire going flat on the road. He didn't say a word when I finished. I was just about to ask if he was there when he said slowly and clearly, "Tell your father not to bother coming in. We won't need him anymore."

I put the phone down without saying good-bye. "You're fired," I told Dad.

14

Slow Learner

On the way home from Dad's, it was Grace who did the speeding. I pedaled slowly, shaking my head over and over. Whatever Dad wanted to do he just did. He never thought of consequences until it was too late. He never learned. I couldn't believe it.

When we reached our street, there was no traffic so Grace fell back to ride beside me. By her scrunched-up face, I knew she'd been thinking too. "Does your Dad pay support money for you?" she wanted to know.

"Beats me," I said.

"Well, will your mom be mad that he lost his job?"

"Wait a minute! Wait a minute!" I wanted to grab her handlebars, but all I managed to do was bump into her front tire.

She swerved to steady herself. "Take it easy."

"Listen," I said, "don't ever, ever mention my dad losing his job, not ever. Not around my mom."

"All right, but won't she find out?"

"Not unless someone tells her. If she does find out, I don't get to see him again."

We had arrived at my house, and we both got off our

111

bikes to wheel them onto the sidewalk. "Don't worry, I won't say anything around your mom." She had turned to go home when she must have remembered something. "Oh, is your class going to the TV station?"

"McManus hasn't said anything about it."

"Brewster has. He said the whole sixth grade is going. Anyone in our room who makes a peep gets a mark on the board. Five marks and you get left behind in the library. Clayton has three marks against him already. I think Brewster tries to get him in trouble."

"McManus isn't like that," I said. "She isn't into blackmail."

"Lucky you. Maybe she'll tell you about the field trip tomorrow. See ya in the morning."

The next day Mrs. McManus did tell us about the field trip. After she took roll she passed out yellowed copies of *Scope* magazine. The date on the cover was May 2, 1974. Russell was pointing this out to everyone when Mrs. McManus nodded. "I know this is an old issue, but the TV play in it is humorous and I think you'll enjoy it. We're starting a new unit on communication. We'll be doing this play, writing a class newspaper, and visiting a TV station. How does that sound to you?"

"Aw right!" we all said together.

Judy raised her hand. After Mrs. McManus called on her, Judy asked, "When are we going to the TV station?"

"A week from Wednesday. We'll need about six of your parents to drive. You can be asking them to vol-

112

unteer while we're getting the play ready for production. When we go on our field trip, you'll see what it would be like to be on TV."

"I wish we were," Pete whispered to me. Pete liked acting in plays almost as much as I did.

"Now," Mrs. McManus went on, "I'll give you some time to skim over *A Man Called Smart*. You can choose the character you'd like to try out for. There are eighteen parts. Some of you might rather make props or paint scenery."

"I'm going to paint scenery," Summer mumbled from the seat in front of me.

She'd be good at that, but I wanted a lead. I read as fast as I could through the play to find out which characters had the most lines. Max, the Chief, and Bediyoskin were main characters. So was 99, but she was a girl.

Max was the one I wanted to be. He was a dingy spy who carried a briefcase that turned into a ladder, a gun, a flashlight, and a parachute. He made dumb mistakes, like pointing his briefcase gun at his own chest when he tried to stick up a KAOS agent, but he always got his man.

"I think most of you have read far enough to decide on a part," Mrs. McManus said. "We'll start with the rows by the windows and read a few pages aloud and then the middle rows can try out. Listen carefully because the class will vote for the players after everyone has had an opportunity to read."

Eric was the first one to play Max. He stumbled on most of his lines. I was next. I thought I was pretty

113

good. The kids laughed. After I finished, I saw Pete
hurriedly look back over the play.

He told Mrs. McManus that he was trying out for the
Chief. That was a good part for him. Russell sits over
by the wall and he was the last one to try out for Max.
He hammed it up too much. Only a couple of kids
laughed.

We voted on 99 first. She's Max's girlfriend. Kate
got the part. Pete was chosen to be the Chief.

After we put our heads down to vote for Max, I
raised my hand for myself. I figure every vote counts. I
don't know how many other kids raised their hands for
me, but I got to be Max.

That's all we did on the play for Monday. By the
next Monday, Pete and I had our lines memorized. We
could pretend we were actually talking on the phone
because we didn't need to read from the magazines
like the rest of the cast did. From the way Mrs. Mc-
Manus smiled at us, I knew she was pleased.

Mrs. McManus told us only five parents had volun-
teered to drive on the field trip. She was sure we'd
need six drivers. My dad still didn't have a job. I
thought a minute before offering to ask him. I didn't
want to miss visiting the TV station, but I knew he
should be looking for work.

I called him after school, half hoping he wouldn't
answer. He didn't. Good. He must have been job
hunting. He was home after dinner. "You busy on
Wednesday?" I asked him.

"I don't have to be," he said. "What's up?"

I told him about the communication unit and the
play and the trip to the station.

114

He congratulated me on getting a lead part. He knew I was a chip off the old block because he was a pretty good actor too. I had to give it to him there.

"We can get five kids in the Camaro," he said. "What time do you want me to meet you at school?"

"We're supposed to leave at two. We're not coming back to school after the field trip, so you'll have to take everybody home."

"No problem," he said. "I'll meet you in your room at five to two."

He was right on time. Mrs. McManus introduced the parents to each other. They talked about the windy March weather while Mrs. McManus sorted the kids into six groups. That morning she'd let the students who had a parent driving choose two friends to ride with them. I chose Pete and then, because Summer had turned around to watch me with such a pitiful look on her face, I chose her too.

Mrs. McManus added Russell to my group. I could have done without him. While Pete and I lagged behind with Summer, Dad slapped Russell on the back and said, "Let's go, son."

I rode in the front seat with Dad. He entertained us with sick jokes most of the way to the TV station. Russell laughed the hardest.

When we were pulling into the parking lot, Dad said to me, "See if you can find a butt in the ashtray. I left my pack at home."

I pulled out the ashtray, hoping I couldn't find one. It'd be embarrassing to have Dad smoking a butt around the other parents. "Nothing's here but ashes," I told him.

He swore under his breath. I was thinking that maybe he hadn't left his cigarettes at home. Maybe he was broke. I took a quick glance at the gas gauge. Fortunately, it was at the halfway mark.

On the first floor of the TV station there were two rows of glassed-in offices. The attendant who herded us around pointed out the anchor people who were inside typing on their computers. We met Grace's class on our way downstairs.

Mrs. McManus let us mill around asking questions. Mr. Brewster had his students in silent military formation. Grace wrinkled her face in disgust as I passed her on the stairs with a knowing grin. I checked for Clayton, but he wasn't there.

The station's basement looked like a large warehouse. One wall was sectioned off into five screened sets. "This is where the cooking demonstrations you see on TV are shot," our attendant said, pointing out a long counter with two ovens behind it. "And a talk show will take place over here in about a half hour."

The camera people were already setting up in front of the raised platform. I imagined myself sitting in one of the armchairs with a camera angled on me. It'd be too cool.

"I'd sure like to be on TV," I said to Mrs. McManus when we were going back up the stairs.

"Maybe you will someday," she said. "You'd be very good at it."

With her compliment reverberating in my head, I floated out to the Camaro with the other kids. Summer was saying she wished we could have seen a live show.

Russell said he wished we could have looked through the cameras.

"Anyway, it was a neat TV station," Pete said, climbing into the backseat with Summer and Russell.

As soon as Dad started up the car, Russell poked him in the shoulder. "Can you stop at a grocery store somewhere, Mr. Johnson? My dad gave me five dollars to buy us kids ice-cream bars."

"No problem," Dad told him. "As soon as we get off the freeway I'll stop at the first place we see."

We didn't see a grocery store until we got to Snohomish. Dad pulled into the parking lot and we all piled out of the car. Inside the store we crowded around the frozen-food cases trying to decide what we could get for five dollars. Summer was willing to settle for Popsicles. Russell wasn't.

We'd finally agreed on a six-pack of ice-cream sandwiches when I realized Dad was missing. "I'll go hunt him up while you guys get in line," I said.

He wasn't in any of the first three aisles. I'd just passed the meat counter and was halfway up aisle four when I spotted him standing by the tobacco case. What I saw him doing there sank my heart to my feet.

He had a carton of cigarettes in his hand and was looking toward the checkout stands. He must have thought he was in the clear because he slid the carton inside the front of his jacket. Automatically I turned to check behind me.

A clerk wheeling a box of paper towels had come to a halt and was staring down the aisle at Dad. When the clerk saw me watching him, he backed up his cart and disappeared. I zipped after Dad.

117

"Young man, weren't you taught any manners?" An old lady touched my shoulder as I tried to maneuver around her and her pile of groceries. I gave her cart a shove so I could get to the express lane. Russell, Pete, and Summer were in line behind a pigtailed woman and her baby. Dad was beside them, nonchalantly leaning against the candy display.

I pulled on his sleeve. "Come here a minute."

He flicked up the four fingers of his right hand, letting me know everything was cool. To make him understand that it wasn't, I jabbed him with my elbow and jerked my head toward the aisle. He just gave me another flick of his hand.

By the perplexed frown on her forehead, I could tell Summer was trying to figure out what was going on. I searched my mind for another silent way to get through to Dad while the clerk handed the pigtailed lady her package and reached out for Russell's box of ice-cream sandwiches. Desperate, I turned my face away from Summer and kneed Dad in the leg, but his attention wasn't on me.

He was eyeing the clerk who was giving Russell his change. When Russell, Pete, and Summer headed for the doors, Dad straightened up and casually followed them out of the grocery store. I stayed on his heels whispering, "Dad, wait. Please wait."

Just as we hit the curb and I was about to yank on the back of his jacket, a man swished past me, grabbed Dad by the arm, and said, "I would like you to return to the store with me."

Dad frowned as if he couldn't figure out what the man was doing. "What's your problem?"

118

"You know what the problem is. Let's get this over without a fuss."

I saw Dad narrow his eyes as he evaluated his position, shrug his shoulders as he decided the jig was up, and turn to go with the man. Panic shot through me. I wanted to scream at the man, shove him away from Dad, yell at Dad to run for it, but I stood helplessly while they walked back up the curb and through the automatic glass doors of the grocery store.

15

Worst Fears

I hurried across the concrete driveway. Pete had turned around at the edge of the parking lot and was facing me. Russell and Summer had stopped with him. "Hey," Pete said, "where's your dad?"

My brain shifted to automatic, riding over my panic. "A little problem came up. Dad's not going to be able to take us home. I'll have to call my mom to come get us. Russell, have you got twenty-five cents left?"

Russell fished a quarter out of his jeans, and before Pete could think up any more questions I made a dive for the phone booth that was on the outside wall of the grocery store. My hand shook as I pushed in the buttons of the number of Patrick's Grill.

The kids gathered outside the phone booth after I finished talking to Mom. "She'll be here in about twenty minutes," I said.

Summer was watching me closely. I knew she knew I was hiding something. I unwrapped the ice-cream sandwich Russell gave me and leaned against the wall of the booth, pretending Dad's disappearance was no

121

big deal. Pete had finished his ice cream and was looking at the box in Russell's hand.

Russell held the box out. "You want one?"

"If nobody else does," Pete said.

"Not me," I said. Summer shook her head. Pete and
Russell shared the last two sandwiches and I was glad.
Eating would keep their minds occupied.

I made my ice cream last as long as possible. I even
licked the foil when I was done. "Here, I'll dump the
stuff in the garbage." I took the box from Russell and
gathered up the wrappings. As I carried the box over
to the waste bin, I shot a glance at my watch. I'd told
Mom to make it as fast as she could. She shouldn't be
longer than seven more minutes.

Summer was standing on one foot and then the
other when I got back. A cold wind was pouring in
from the street. "Where'd your dad have to go?" Pete
asked. "His car's still in the lot."

"Wow!" Russell's attention was on the entrance of
the parking lot. "The cops are here."

Two police cars nosed onto the concrete lot and
stopped in front of the grocery's automatic doors.
Without speaking to each other, the cops jumped out
of their cars at the same second and marched into the
store together.

"Jeez." Russell's brown eyes were opened wide.
"What's going on?"

I leaned forward on my toes as if I'd spotted something in the street beyond the parking lot. "I think I
see Mom. Come on, let's go."

"No, let's wait until she drives up here," Russell
said. "I wanna see what's happening."

122

I pushed Summer forward. "Mom gets mad if she has to wait. We better get out there."

Summer and Pete moved to the curb with me, but Russell stayed stubbornly by the phone booth. Before we got to the edge of the parking lot, Pete narrowed his eyes into slits while he scanned the street. "I don't see your mom's car."

The light must have changed and thinned the traffic. As I watched a Buick and truck move out of sight, I prayed desperately for Mom to come. Just as Pete turned to join Russell, the old gray Camaro appeared on the side road. Tears of relief filled my eyes. "Hey, she's here! Let's go, you guys."

But it was too late. Russell was pointing to a cop coming from the side of the store. Following him came Dad. And right on Dad's heels was the second cop.

I heard Summer take in a breath. I heard Pete murmur, "No." I couldn't hear what Dad was saying to the policemen, but he was acting like he was chatting with old buddies, like it was no big thing that there were handcuffs on his wrists.

Mom pulled up in front of us and opened the passenger door. "Get in, kids."

I got in the front seat quickly. Summer and Pete climbed in back. Russell slowly crossed over to us with his eyes riveted on Dad, who was being put in the first patrol car.

Russell had barely gotten the door closed on his side when Mom shifted into reverse and backed out into the road. She didn't say a word as she turned onto the main street and down toward Pete's house. I kept my eyes focused on the windshield, although the only thing I could see was the image of Dad bending into the police car with his hands locked behind him.

When Mom stopped at Pete's house, Russell got out with him. "I can walk home from here," he told Mom.

Pete said, "Thanks for the ride, Mrs. Johnson."

Neither of them said anything to me and I didn't say anything to them. I was keeping my eyes straight ahead. Summer gave Mom the directions to her house. When we got there, Summer touched me on my arm before she jumped out. "Bye, Jerry."

I didn't answer her.

By the time we arrived home, my face was wet from crying. Mom turned off the engine and sat looking at me. "Honey, there's nothing we can do about him. That's just the way he is."

I smeared the tears away from my chin with my sleeve. "Why'd they need two cop cars? Didn't they have anything else to do? It doesn't take two cars to pick up a shoplifter."

"What'd he steal?"

"A stupid carton of cigarettes. He was out of butts."

"What a waste." She clicked her tongue against her teeth as she shook her head. "Well, there's nothing we can do now. Do you want to come down to the restaurant with me?"

"No."

"Fix you up with a good meal."

"No. I don't need sympathy."

She turned the key in the ignition. "Maybe I need to be with you."

"Sure. You divorced him."

"What did you think I should do?"

124

"Get rid of him," I said, and got out of the car and went into the house.

I didn't have any intention of going to school in the morning. I stayed in bed listening to the yelling coming from the house next door. Pete had no doubt told his mom about Dad and Mrs. McCartney had no doubt called Mrs. Elliott and now Mrs. Elliott was no doubt laying the law down to Grace.

Mom opened my bedroom door. "On your feet, Jerry. Breakfast is ready."

"I'm not going to school."

"Yes, you are. You have to go to school sometime and it might as well be today. Putting it off isn't going to make it any easier."

I looked over my blankets at her. "Every kid in the school will know."

She looked steadily back at me. "They probably will. But the faster you face them the better. Get up right now."

She closed the door and I dragged myself out of bed.

Grace caught up with me when I was halfway to the bus stop. "Hey! How come you left without me?"

I glanced sideways at her. "How come your face is all puffy?"

"Mom was screaming at me."

"I bet."

"Everything's okay now." Grace grabbed onto my jacket, trying to slow me down. "Dad told her we shouldn't have to be separated because of what your father did."

"That was big of the Reverend."

She gave my jacket a yank. "Come on. You know my mom. There's nothing I can do about her."

I slowed down. There was nothing I could do about what my dad did either, except cringe as the bus approached our stop.

"Don't worry. The kids will forget about it after a couple days," Grace said before we climbed on the bus and rode off to school.

I walked into the classroom like a zombie, keeping my attention on the floor. Summer turned around as I slid into my seat.

"Face the front," I told her.

"I'm sorry about your dad," she whispered.

I took my math book out, flipped to a page of division problems, and stared at them until she turned back around.

Mrs. McManus started first period with a geography test. I didn't care where the Washington State cities were. I put my dots any old place on the map. I was just glad the room was quiet and nobody was looking at me.

When recess time came, Pete asked Kathy, the class monitor, for a ball and bat. I thought that meant we'd play together like always, but when I moved toward him he zipped out the door and caught up with Eric and Robert. I dropped back into the room and asked Kathy for a library pass.

After recess Mrs. McManus had us rehearse the play in front of the backdrop Summer and Judy had painted. Pete stood as far away from me as he could when we had our scenes together. He didn't even get close when he was supposed to be pulling me out of a revolving door. Mrs. McManus acted like she didn't notice.

She assigned us twenty sentences using adverbs when the rehearsal was over. I spent the period staring at my blank paper. I couldn't breathe normally and my face wouldn't cool down. I'd had nightmares about kids finding out about my dad. It's worse when it happens, though.

On the way home from school Grace asked me how my day went. "How do you think it went?" I asked her back.

When I got to my house, I saw Mom and a bald-headed man coming out of the garage. "Willard," Mom said, taking the man's arm, "this is my son, Jerry."

As soon as we'd shaken hands Willard took off toward Mom's car. "What's the talkative old geezer doing here?" I wanted to know.

"Keep your voice down!" Mom said sharply. "He's the new owner of the restaurant. He helped me bring your dad's car home. I have to drive him back, but it won't take me long. How was your day?"

"Pukey. What'd you expect?" I went on into the garage to look at the black Camaro. At first I ran my hand over the sleek hood. Then as my day came up in my throat, I gave it a hard punch. I'd never hurt my kid like my dad hurt me. I would never be like him.

16

True Believers

Pete had the wastebasket beside his desk and was dumping his old crumpled papers in it when I got to class the next morning. Russell came over to stand near him. "Your folks moving?"

"No," Pete said. "I'm transferring into Brewster's room."

Russell's fat lips curled away from his teeth. "What for, man? That room's the pits."

"My mother doesn't think so. Excuse me." Pete stood up, pushed Russell out of the way, and went up the aisle with the basket.

After he'd plunked it down beside Mrs. McManus's desk, she gave him a large manila envelope. "These are your test papers and an estimate of your grades so far this semester, Pete. We're going to miss you."

Pete bobbed his head at her, took the envelope to his desk, placed it on top of his books, and carried the whole stack out the door with him.

Summer twisted around in her seat to take a peek at me.

129

"Face the front!" I snarled. I didn't feel sorry about making her mouth quiver. She was a baby anyway.

All the time Mrs. McManus was calling roll, I was drumming my fingers under the edge of my desk. What was I going to do? What was I going to do? Nobody was going to play ball with me. I couldn't spend recess in the library for the rest of the year. Every muscle in my body wanted me to spring up and take off.

"Since Pete has transferred into Mr. Brewster's room," Mrs. McManus was saying, "we'll have to have a new Chief of Spies."

My heart thumped. The kids were probably wishing I'd drop out of the play. I raised my hand.

"Yes?" Mrs. McManus said to me.

"I quit as Max Smart."

She looked confused. "Do you want to be the Chief?"

"No, I just think I shouldn't be in the play."

"That's ridiculous," she said. "You're marvelous as Max Smart."

The whole class was staring at me, and it was impossible to think of what to say next while my muscles were urging, Split, split.

Mrs. McManus walked over to the blackboard. "Those of you who want to try out for the Chief raise your hands and I'll put your names on the board. We'll have free reading this morning and you can go over the Chief's lines then. The tryouts will be just before lunch."

Eric won the Chief's part. He still stumbled over his

130

lines, but Russell overacted and Robert was so stiff he killed all the gags.

I went to the library again during lunch recess. Part of the time I flipped through the pages of a book about how things work. I usually liked this book, but I couldn't keep my mind on generators and engines while I heard the kids shouting out on the playground.

When I put the book back on the shelf by the windows, I looked outside. At first all I saw was our class playing baseball down in the left field. Then Brewster came into sight from around the school building with his class marching behind him. Grace's face was knotted into a murderous scowl as she tramped to Brewster's military count. Clayton was staring squint-eyed at Brewster's back as if he were measuring for a knife throw. I couldn't see Pete's face because his head was hanging down. I hoped he was enjoying his recess.

"What were you guys doing at noon?" I asked Grace on the way home from school.

"Brewster was making True Believers out of us. A couple kids peeped during the math quiz so he said we'd march every recess until we learned how to behave during a test." Grace wasn't scowling anymore. She had that inward look of someone who was plotting to do someone in. "True Believers! Ha. Wait until my mother hears he said that!"

"You figure it'll get you out of Brewster's room?"

"Sure." She jumped up and batted the branches of a cedar tree whose limbs were hanging over the sidewalk. "And since Pete's transferred in, our room has more kids than yours does."

Grace took a quick glance at me after she said Pete's

name. "Look, Jerry. That stuff about your dad will blow over. Somebody will get conked with a baseball and that'll be the hot topic of conversation."

"Do all the kids in your room know about my dad?"

"Of course. But it's just today's news. It'll get old."

"It's going to get pretty old not having friends," I shot back.

"Not everyone's like Pete's mom."

"Not even your mom?" I knew I shouldn't be taking my bitterness out on Grace, but I couldn't stop myself.

Her good mood wilted. Instead of jumping for tree branches she chewed on her thumbnail. "My mom," Grace said slowly, "will remember to be a good Christian."

That was too much for me. I didn't want to be anyone's lost lamb. "See ya, PK," I said, and sprinted for home.

About five o'clock Saturday I got a frantic call from Mom. "Jerry," she said, "the busboy who works my station just quit. Can you please come down and bus tables for me?"

"I don't know anything about busing tables," I told her.

"All you have to do is clean the tables, set the tables, and pour water into glasses. Any idiot can do that."

"Thanks, Mom."

"Listen, honey, the restaurant's packed and I'm running my legs off. Come on down and earn some money."

"Money?" I said. "I'll be on the next bus. What do I wear?"

"A clean white shirt, and hurry. Good-bye."

Busing tables wasn't bad. Before the night was over I was swishing menus into the customers' hands and saying, "Your waitress this evening will be Lily. She'll be here to take your order in a moment."

Willard, who was working the cash register, seemed to get off on watching me. I didn't get off on his idea of pay, though.

"That old buzzard gave me five bucks for four hours work," I told Mom on our drive home.

She fumbled in the pocket of her uniform while still keeping an eye on the road. "Here, take some of my tip money. I usually share it with the busboy anyway."

She handed over another five bucks. "Your dad called today. Do you want to go see him tomorrow?"

"He never wanted me to see him in prison before."

She had stopped for a red light and was looking over at me. "I think he wants to apologize to you."

"Forget that."

"He is your dad."

"Some dad." I poked my finger toward the light. "How green do you want it to get?"

Even with the ten dollars in my jeans, I hated waking up Monday morning. I could barely pull myself out of bed to get ready for school. If I were sixteen, I could work full-time. I'd gotten a blast out of making the customers smile by raising the pitcher up two feet and pouring water into their glasses as if it were coming from a waterfall. I'd like always to have a job and money in my jeans.

It was another day of shame at the school I couldn't

133

stand. Summer didn't say hi to me before I slid into my seat. I guess she'd learned her lesson. All the time I was doing math and geography, I was miserably aware of Pete's empty desk beside me. I'd guessed it would be that way for the rest of the semester, so when Clayton and Mrs. Nettle walked into our classroom, my back stiffened.

"Here's a new student for you," Mrs. Nettle said to Mrs. McManus.

Mrs. McManus was writing our English assignment on the board. She put down her chalk to welcome Clayton. "We're glad to have you. I've heard that you're a very bright student."

I bet that wasn't all she'd heard, but she didn't seem to see the peace symbol dangling from Clayton's left ear. She told him to take the empty seat in the fifth row. Clayton dumped his books on Pete's desk, gave me a grin, and sat down. After he'd stowed his books away, he folded his arms behind his head, stretched, and then asked, "When's lunch?"

"In three minutes," I said.

I worried for three minutes about whether or not I should try to be friendly during lunchtime. I didn't need another "get lost" message. I decided to play it cool and just answer questions if Clayton asked me any.

He did as soon as he brought his lunch tray in from the hall. "What do you guys play at recess?"

"Some kids play basketball or baseball. I usually read."

"You do?" He stared at me as if that was the nerdiest thing he'd ever heard.

I concentrated on my chicken sandwich until lunch was over and I could scuttle off to the library.

PE was the hour I dreaded most. It was sunny outside and Mr. Tada was sure to take us out for baseball. What if nobody chose me? What if I were the last one chosen and left way out in the field somewhere while everyone else took part in the action?

I was almost sick by the time English was over and Mrs. McManus marched us into the gym. I thought of asking her to let me go to the nurse's room. But I didn't ask, and when Mr. Tada announced that we'd go out in the sunshine for a baseball game, I felt even sicker.

It was Russell and Judy's turn to be captains. Judy went first and chose Kate. Russell chose Robert. Judy called out Wayne's name. Russell called out mine, but it didn't register in my ears. I was busy kicking a hole in the playground gravel.

"Johnson!" Russell hollered.

Clayton gave me a shove forward.

"Oh, I was spacing out." I hurried over to stand by Russell.

Eric is the least coordinated of the boys and Russell called his name last. Summer was the last one Judy chose. Summer doesn't like to play with her glasses on and she can't see a ball coming right at her with her glasses off.

"Robert, you pitch," Russell ordered. "And Denise, you catch. Jerry, you take first base and Beth second and Eddie third and Clayton shortstop and the rest of you guys go out in the field with me."

I picked up a mitt and a bag from the equipment cart

and trotted over to put the bag on first base. I felt as if I were in some kind of movie. That this wasn't really happening. I'd smashed Russell's face in and he still let me play first base and put himself in the field?

"Play ball!" Mr. Tada yelled.

Judy went up to bat. Robert put the ball over the plate. Judy swung. The ball bounced once. Clayton stepped forward, caught it, zoomed it to me. I crouched to tag Judy as she slid for the base.

Mr. Tada jerked his thumb over his shoulder. "You're out!"

Russell leaped into the air. "Way to go, Johnson. We'll shut them out."

We didn't, though. Our team was sharper in the field, but Kate has a stronger pitching arm than Robert has. Mr. Tada stopped the game when it was 4 to 3, our favor.

Before we went in, Russell gathered our team in a victory circle, and we tossed our mitts in the air. Clayton trotted beside me on the way back to the gym. "How come you read during recess?"

"I don't have to anymore," I told him.

17

I'll See You on TV Someday

Grace tipped back in our kitchen chair. "Ah," she said. "My big afternoon off."

"Your mom ever gets home early from her meeting and finds you inside my house, you'll spend Tuesdays chained in your yard."

"She'll never catch me. What's in your mail?"

"Junk." I was sorting the bills into one pile on the table and the advertisements into another when his envelope came up. I stared at the handwriting a second, feeling anger rush to my head. Then I walked over to the sink, opened the cabinet door below, and dropped the letter in the garbage pail.

"What are you doing?" Grace asked.

"Putting garbage in the garbage."

Grace clunked down her chair and got the letter out of the pail. "Jerry, this is from your dad."

"I know it is and it will say, 'My boy, I love you,' and that's a bunch of garbage."

"How come he's in prison? Matt said shoplifting isn't a felony and they usually just fine you or make you do community service."

137

"But my dad broke parole again and the prosecutor has the right to dump him back in the system. He has to finish his whole sentence for car theft this time. So your brother doesn't know everything, and throw the letter away. I'm not going to read it."

Grace stood there, wiping the back of the envelope across her pant leg. "Your dad's nice in some ways. He's friendly and funny and generous and—"

"And a thief. You don't know anything about what it's like to be a thief's son, PK."

"My life isn't perfect, Jerry Johnson, and neither is my dad. Mom says he pays more attention to other families' problems than he does to ours."

"Poor little you." I zipped up my jacket. "Let's go bike riding, and throw that thing away or I'll throw it away for you."

"No, you won't." Grace marched over to the refrigerator and slapped the letter on top of it. "Now, where do you want to go?"

"Let's ride up to Avenue D and get some milk shakes."

"I don't have any money."

"I do. And I need a candy bar for a friend."

"Who's the friend?" Grace asked as she went past me and out the back door.

"That's a good question," I said, locking the door behind us.

After we had our milk shakes, we stopped at Safeway and I picked out four large mint patties. Before we rolled our bikes down the Safeway lot, I handed one to Grace, took the silver foil off one for me, and put the others in my jacket pocket.

138

"Who's the friend?" Grace asked again.

I raised one eyebrow at her. "So, Clayton aced you out of coming into McManus's class."

"My mom didn't make it to the school until after Clayton's mom had already been there." Grace bit into her candy as if she wished it were her mother. "Mrs. Nettle said there was a personality conflict between Clayton and Mr. Brewster, but there wasn't any valid reason for me to get transferred since Brewster hadn't disciplined me again."

I took a bite of my candy. The sharp mint filling slid down my throat and left the sweet dark chocolate sticking to my teeth. I tongued it loose while we steered our bikes out of the Safeway parking lot. "Does Clayton know my dad was picked up by the cops?"

"Of course. But nobody cares about that anymore. Mrs McCartney's been on the phone to my dad every night trying to find a cheap church school. Pete keeps complaining about losing his recesses and she's going to put him in a private school if Mr. Brewster doesn't stop marching us around."

"What did Mrs. Nettle say about Brewster making you guys True Believers?"

"She said she'd have a talk with him. A lot of good that will do. He'll just think up some other army tactic." We'd reached Avenue D, and Grace hopped on her bike. "My mom thinks it's worse for a boy to lose his recess than it is for a girl."

"Ya, poor Pete." I raced home ahead of Grace, letting the March wind blow into the grin on my face.

The grin melted off after I walked past Dad's black

Camaro to park my bike in the garage. The car reminded me of his cruddy letter on top of the refrigerator. I didn't have the guts to read it and I didn't have the guts to dump it in the garbage again. I went in the house and headed straight for my bedroom without stopping in the kitchen.

The next morning at school, Summer tipped her head down after she saw me coming in the door. I dropped a mint patty on her library book. Her green eyes widened. "Is this for me?"

"It's on your desk, isn't it?"

"Thanks a lot. I'll eat it after lunch." When Summer smiles, it makes me think of sunshine. Maybe that's how she got her name.

I had a mint patty at noon too. Clayton watched me eat it. "Man, that looks good."

I broke off a piece and handed it to him. He slouched down in his seat and ate it slowly, licking his fingers when he was done. "This room sure beats Brewster's. All we could do at lunch was read a book, silently. Brewster loves silence."

Kathy threw her empty lunch sack in the tall wastebasket in front of the room, picked up the library passes, and moved over by the equipment box.

Clayton put up his hand. "Raise your hand too," he told me, "so we can get the bat and ball."

We came back in from lunch recess sticky with sweat. Most of the time it rains in the spring, but when the sun does come out it really beats on you. Especially if you're racing around bases and sliding after balls.

I pulled my soaked T-shirt away from my chest and

140

Clayton mopped his flushed face with his sleeve while Mrs. McManus gave us the word about the play production. She'd invited Mrs. Nettle and two second-grade classes in to see it on Thursday afternoon. She thought the little children would enjoy it very much and it would be good for us to experience an audience.

When she finished with her announcement, she told us to get out our arithmetic books and do the problems on page 147. I got my book out slowly. Second-graders, huh? Mrs. McManus must know about my dad and was playing it safe by inviting little kids. I wouldn't want Pete in the audience, but I hated the idea of teachers whispering and planning behind my back.

By Thursday morning I was excited about the play anyway. Mom had bought me a tie and borrowed a suit jacket from one of the waiters so I'd look the part of Max, the counterspy. I could feel the excitement of the other kids as we milled around the room, admiring each other's costumes.

"All right, class, that's the last bell. Settle down," Mrs. McManus ordered.

She took roll and then passed out another geography test. We all groaned. This wasn't what we wanted to do on the day of a performance.

I'd just started mapping in the rivers of Washington State when Summer turned around. "I think I've got the flu. I don't feel good," she whispered.

She didn't look good either. Her face was all white except for around her mouth, where it was yellow. "Tell Mrs. McManus," I whispered back.

"Please don't talk during a test," Mrs. McManus said from her desk.

141

Summer raised her left hand. She had her right hand over her mouth.

"Put your hand down," Mrs. McManus said. "I can't answer questions during a test."

Summer turned around to me again with both hands over her mouth. Her body was making little jerks. I slid as far away from her as I could, waved my hand frantically, and called out, "Mrs. McManus, Mrs.—"

It was too late. A stream of vomit shot through Summer's fingers and poured across my test paper and down my desk. I leaped out of my seat, knocked into Clayton, who leaped out of his seat and yelled, "Jeez, what a stink!"

Mrs. McManus rushed over to Summer and tried to hurry her out of the room, but every few steps Summer doubled up and puked on the floor. "Kathy, get the janitor," Mrs. McManus ordered. Kathy made a wide circle around Summer before zipping out the door.

It took the janitor two pails of water and one pail of sawdust to clean up Summer's mess. When Mrs. McManus came back, she opened the windows and gave me a new test paper. I sat down to draw the rivers of Washington State all over again.

By the afternoon our room was aired out. The second-graders wouldn't have cared if it still stunk. They thought the play was hilarious. A little yellow-haired boy laughed so hard, he fell out of his chair.

After our bows, Mrs. Nettle stood up. "I'm terribly proud of this troupe of players. Today you made other children happy. Today you did a generous thing."

142

Then she looked right at me with a big smile. "Jerry, I want to make a prediction about you. I predict that I'll see you on TV someday."

"Sure, in a police lineup." It was Russell's voice coming from the back of the room.

My face burned. Mrs. Nettle's face turned to stone, but she didn't move her head or change her voice. "Will Miss Lee's second-graders file out first, please."

When all the little kids had left and we had shoved our desks back in place, Mrs. Nettle walked across the room, took Russell's arm in an iron grip, and hauled him out the door. Clayton watched them go, muttering, "That guy will do anything to get attention."

I told the whole story to Grace on the way home from school. "What'd you expect from Russell?" she asked.

"I thought he might be turning into a nice guy. He chose me to be on his team."

"That doesn't make him a nice guy. You're one of the best ball players in sixth grade. Of course he chose you to be on his team."

All the rest of the way to my house, while Grace chattered away, I kept poking around inside my head to find out if Russell's crack hurt me. I guess it didn't because I could only hear Mrs. Nettle's voice: *I'll see you on TV someday.*

Mom was rushing around in her bedroom when I got home. "What's up?" I asked her.

"Honey, I'm going out to a show and dinner. There's not much food in the house so I'll have to give you money to ride your bike up to McDonald's. And I saw your dad's letter on top of the fridge. Aren't you going to read it?"

"What's the point of reading it?"

She didn't have an answer for that.

I leaned against the bedpost, watching her peer into the mirror while she put on green glass earrings. "So, who's taking you to dinner?"

"Willard. There's the door. Go let him in."

"Willard? You got to be kidding."

"Jerry, please. Be nice."

I let the buzzard in. He was wearing a cap on his bald head. "Hi," I said. "You going golfing?"

"No." He took his cap off and sat down on the couch.

I sat down in the big chair. "How's the restaurant?"

"Fine."

"Did you hire a new busboy?"

"Yes."

"How's he working out?"

Willard shrugged.

"Ah. Um. Mom's almost ready. She'll be out in a minute."

Willard nodded and twirled his cap.

I was out of ideas for conversation. How do you talk to this old guy?

Mom bustled into the room with a shiny smile for Willard. "We won't be too late," she said to me as she fumbled around in her purse. "Darn, I've only got three dollars. I'll have to get some more out of my other coat."

Before she could leave for her bedroom, Willard asked, "Where's he going?"

"He probably wants to go to McDonald's."

"Three dollars is plenty for McDonald's." Willard placed his cap firmly on his bald head.

Mom gave me the three dollars, a quick kiss, and followed Willard out the front door.

So now I knew what made Willard talk. Money.

I checked inside the fridge. Mom was right. Hardly anything in it. Her mind must not have been on grocery shopping. I cracked open a can of Pepsi, took it into the living room, and switched on the TV. Talk shows. I switched off the TV and settled crossways in the big chair.

I didn't like the way Mom kowtowed to Willard. Three dollars for my dinner? If Mom was planning to marry him for his money, she'd have a fat chance of getting any of it. The thought of life with stingy, silent Willard had me crushing the empty Pepsi can in my hands.

My dad wasn't stingy. But he had sticky fingers. And couldn't keep a straight job. I wished I could cut those parts out of him and just leave him funny and friendly and warm and . . .

Before I knew what I was doing, I'd gotten up from my chair, dumped the crushed can in the kitchen garbage, and grabbed Dad's letter off the top of the refrigerator.

"Dear son," his letter began. "I waited around all Sunday hoping Lily would bring you up here. Sunday night I cried in my bunk. I don't blame you for not coming. I can hardly stand myself for doing what I did.

"They strip you of everything in prison. All you can try to hold on to is your self-respect. I haven't even got that after hurting you. I hate myself so much my knuckles are bloody from driving my fist into the cell wall.

"I told Lily that as soon as they give me a job I'll send her money so you two can move. I know how kids are and your life must be a nightmare. I feel like a jerk even saying I love you. Please don't hate me too much. Yr Dad."

I took in some long breaths after I finished his letter. Half an hour went by while I sat at the kitchen table and thought of his bloody knuckles and if I wanted to write him back. I knew he'd probably always be a loser, but I couldn't keep hating him. And there was no use making him feel sadder just because I felt sad that he couldn't keep his promises.

When I had a letter mapped in my mind, I got a pen and paper from my school folder and started out. "Dear Dad, Don't worry. We don't have to move because I've still got three friends left. Only one of them puked all over my desk today. See, we were taking this geography test and . . ."

Barthe DeClements is the author of several award-winning novels for children and young adults, including the best-selling *Nothing's Fair in Fifth Grade* and *Sixth Grade Can Really Kill You*. In addition to her writing, she has also worked as a psychologist, a teacher, and a school counselor. Her most recent novel for Delacorte Press was *Five-Finger Discount,* also available in a Dell Yearling edition.

Barthe DeClements has four grown children and two pet wolf hybrids. She lives in a log house on the Pilchuck River near Snohomish, Washington.